When Evil Surged

A Harvey Hughes Novel

Jamell Ponder

PROLOGUE

Harvey was a good man. He embodied good and hated evil. His parents were staunch bible-thumpers, ignorant of their own fall from grace.

Harvey's father, William once told him, "Evil is real, it lives inside of us and sometimes it wins because we let it." Harvey often labored to decipher his father's words.

Harvey never forgot the scripture his mother, Jean read to him when he was 9: "Behold I was brought forth in iniquity, and in sin my mother conceived me." Conception ensued as he heard his parents pray, "Cleanse us oh God. Create in us a clean heart and renew a steadfast spirit in us."

Harvey chose friends wisely, and selected enemies with involuntary grace. He was loved by many, disliked by some, yet a master of his own demise.

Harvey admired successful people and aspired to be as those he revered. William taught Harvey to respect self and others, the golden rule and what it meant to be a gentleman.

Harvey would one day learn; pain was a part of living, and that life offers choices-usually two. In the face of evil he would unveil the person beneath. Evil would, one day present Harvey with his greatest dilemma: obey his moral compass or succumb to the evil resting within.

CHAPTER 1

Harvey sat perplexed and exhausted behind his piano while waiting for his next student. He had already taught several students in a day which felt endless. Harvey went to the bathroom splashed water on his face and said to himself, "Only one more student, then I can relax." Harvey fixed his hair in the mirror, "Who's there?" He realized he was alone; Not his preferred way of being. Harvey turned to walk back to the music room, "I must really be tired if I'm seeing people that aren't there." He sat on the plush blue couch and laid his head back while waiting for Stephanie and Ariana to arrive.

"Another kid?" Harvey said as he scratched his forehead. He didn't mind teaching children, though adults were sometimes easier if not set in their maladaptive habits.

Harvey's last student of the day canceled, which would make the next student, Ariana, his last. "I really hope

Stephanie is on time bringing Ariana, I can fall asleep right..." Harvey's thought was interrupted by the knocking on the studio door. "It's only 4:40 in the afternoon, who's here?" Harvey walked towards the front door of the studio. He peered through the door's peep hole and to his surprise there stood, who he assumed was, Ariana and her mother, Stephanie.

"Oh, hi there!" Harvey said with excitement as he looked at his watch. Harvey extended his hand, Stephanie obliged. "Well thank you for coming." Harvey said as he exchanged looks between Stephanie and Ariana. "This little girl really reminds me of someone." The transient thought ended as did the handshake.

Stephanie frantically struggled to get her car keys into her pocket, "You're welcome. I know we're early and I'm so sorry. I hope this is alright. It's just that I got out of work a little early and decided to come on over..." Stephanie smiled and ran her right hand gently through her hair. Stephanie was a genuinely kind, considerate and amicable woman; Described by loved ones as virtuous.

"Well today is your lucky day. A couple of students canceled so I was just sitting here preparing for your lesson." Harvey presumed his dry sense of humor was good for lightening the mood, defeating awkwardness per se. "Aren't you glad you get to be lucky today?" Harvey chuckled.

Stephanie smirked, but ultimately ignored Harvey's question. "Okay great and again we're sorry." Stephanie replied. Her people-pleasing curse emerged. She lowered her eyes, embarrassed by her decision to arrive twenty minutes early for Ariana's lesson. Harvey's duty to good emerged, "I am glad you are both here."

Stephanie was impressed with Harvey's professionalism. She inconspicuously acknowledged his impalpable charm

"It's no..." Harvey began saying as he waved his hand slightly to the right as if to presumably waive the offense.

"Okay c'mon guys let's play some music!" Ariana demanded.

"Well, we have certainly been told!" Harvey laughed then stretched his hand towards Stephanie and Ariana, "I realize we never introduced ourselves, forgive me." Harvey shook his head. "Nice to officially meet both of you, I'm Harvey." He showed the smile famous for illuminating hearts.

"Nice to meet you as well, I'm Stephanie, and this is my oh-so-lovely daughter, Ariana." Stephanie returned the smile as she rubbed Ariana's back.

"Oh, I am sure she is so..." Harvey began saying.

"Guys..." Ariana called out, showing her impatience. "Why would a 5-year-old want to hear boring conversation between adults?"

Harvey took a deep breath. "Well then I guess we'd better get to practicing." Harvey responded.

Stephanie looked at Ariana and shook her head with disbelief.

"Right this way." Harvey motioned.

Stephanie, Ariana, and Harvey walked through the door of the small waiting area, down a short hallway and into the piano room.

Stephanie was astonished with Harvey and the establishment he developed at such a young age. The studio wasn't very big, but it was elegant. The short hallway was painted pastel blue with white trim. Visible throughout the studio were professional photographs of world-renowned pianists, both living and deceased. There was a picture of Harvey in concert with a band. The still photo was worth sitting amongst the other legends. Harvey's hair was slightly longer in the picture. The photo depicted energy and passion. They turned left and entered the piano room where Harvey had two baby grand pianos, music books, paper copies of material and a stereo. Musical notes on paper decorated the neutrally colored wall. There were pictures of Harvey's parents with a little girl who appeared to be approximately 4 years old. The picture with Harvey and the little girl told a thousand stories, commemorating one of the happiest days of his life.

"Well let me hear you play something." Harvey said to Ariana.

"I thought I was here for you to teach me." The thing no one could sincerely doubt was Ariana's spirited nature. For such a young child she'd developed quite a knack for sarcasm and wit.

"You are certainly a smart little girl." Harvey laughed. "I want to hear you play so I know where we should start our lessons." His million-dollar smile warmed both Ariana and Stephanie's heart.

"Ha! Ha!" Ariana chuckled, "That's all you had to say. I will play!" Harvey quickly learned that Ariana was direct. He grinned as he thought it would be best to simply smile and nod.

Ariana began to play. Harvey listened and looked with amazement at the talent of this young, novice pianist. Harvey recognized the piece as the famous *Fur Elise* by Beethoven.

Harvey began to clap, "Great job, you certainly are talented. Where did you learn how to play like that?" Harvey asked.

Stephanie smiled. She was proud of her daughter.

"My grandmother has been teaching me." Ariana smiled. She really loved her grandmother.
"She is doing a wonderful job."

Stephanie smiled. "My mother is a wonderful woman." Stephanie thought. She clapped, "Ariana is so talented, and I am proud of my baby." Stephanie's mood seemed incongruent with her statement. "Ariana's dad would be so proud of her as well."

Ariana smiled in response to all the accolades she was receiving.
"Is everything okay Stephanie?" Harvey asked. Stephanie quickly readjusted in her chair, "Yes, yes things are just fine." Stephanie took a deep breath then turned her attention to Ariana, "Hey, Mr. Harvey said some very

nice things about you, what are you going to say to him?"

Ariana giggled, "Oh yeah, I forgot. Thank you, Mr. Harvey."

Harvey and Ariana shared a smile, "You're welcome. So, we are going to work on your understanding of the circle of fifths and knowledge of music theory, chords and use of your bass hand."

"What does that mean?" Ariana asked as she raised her eyebrows slightly.

Bewildered, Stephanie asked, "Um yes, what does that mean exactly?" Though her mother was an accomplished pianist, Stephanie did not inherit the gift.

"No worries, all this will eventually be as clear as mud." Harvey responded with a slight giggle.

The lesson concluded 30 minutes later.

"Well, it was nice to meet both of you. I am looking forward to next week's lesson."

"We are looking forward to the lesson next week also Harvey." Stephanie responded.

"Yes, we are..." Ariana joined with excitement as she bounced up and down.

Harvey walked Stephanie and Ariana to their car; a blue 2014 Kia Sol. "That car seems to fit her!" He thought, "She looks like she belongs in that car. Whatever that means!" He said to himself. "Stephanie is a lovely lady." Harvey said as he walked back inside. "Oh my, what a long day!" He said, inviting darkness as he shut off the lights, closed the door and walked away.

CHAPTER 2

Harvey laid in his bed that night thinking of how pleasant his first meeting was with Stephanie and Ariana.

"That little Ariana certainly has some talent, some pizazz too." Harvey scratched his chin and thought a little while longer. "May be slightly unprofessional, but Stephanie is amazingly beautiful." Stephanie stood about 5 feet 4 inches. She had long, blonde hair with dark highlights. Her face was thin, lips were medium in thickness, and her hips were well curved for her small frame. She had thin and rather long legs when compared to her height. The shape of her body led Harvey to believe she frequented the gym. Her eyes were ocean blue, and her eyebrows were thinly shaped with only a slight curve on the ends closest to the middle of her face. She was easy on the eyes. Overall, she was a stunning beauty with a figure that evoked lustful thoughts.

"I guess I better make sure Ariana continues coming to her lessons…" Harvey paused, "Eh forget it! A girl like her will never go for a guy like me!"

Harvey was kind and patient, fun and smart, but quirky and struggled to understand women. And asking a woman for a date-don't even think about it. Harvey hadn't had a legitimate date in over a year. Harvey rarely expressed emotion. He was sometimes withdrawn and did not have many friends.

Harvey's periodic reclusive nature provided partial explanation for his relatively unmatched skill as a piano player. Harvey was somewhat of a child prodigy-By the age of 15 he had composed his first sonata. While his high school friends listened to the latest pop artists and most popular hip-hop songs of the era, Harvey was moved by jazz legends such as Miles Davis and John Coltrane, and classical pianist like Beethoven, Bach and Mozart.

Everyone always presumed Harvey was different. He would give the shirt off his back and the shoes from his feet to anyone in need. In his second year of college, with the help of a few professors Harvey started a not-for-profit organization, *More for the Least of These*.

Out of the pureness and goodness of his heart he fed many, counseled some and mentored more youth than he could count. The program lasted a year and a half until government funding ceased. And after the government-funded program ended, Harvey still mentored some and delivered food to homeless people. Harvey learned benevolence and compassion from his mother, Suzanne. His father, James taught him a few things as well and they would be certain to surface at some point.

Long before becoming a generous adult, Harvey was an only child with an unhealthy sense of entitlement. He didn't ask for much, but when Harvey did ask, he usually got what he wanted. His parents often wondered if they made a mistake having only one child and indulging many of his desires. It had been a while since Harvey wanted anything, but now the time had come. He wanted not just something, but someone. He wanted Stephanie. He couldn't quite put his finger on why, but he knew there was something about her. He had to get to know more about her. He looked forward to next week's lesson for more reasons than one.

CHAPTER 3

Stephanie went about her week as normal. Harvey traversed her thoughts occasionally. She did her best to ignore them. Though she thought Harvey was kind and handsome, the focus was on her children-Ariana and Johnathan. Stephanie barely had time to think, let alone date.

The piano lesson was nearing the end, and Stephanie began daydreaming about Jeffery. She vividly remembered holding Jeffery's hand and gently caressing his head as he embraced life's final moments.

Jeffery was frail. He attempted various treatment options such as surgery and radiofrequency ablation to destroy his Carcinoid tumor. All attempts were unsuccessful, and Jeffery knew his demise was near.

Eventually Jeffery mustered the strength to say, "I love you and its okay to cry. Please tell Ariana that I love her more than words can express." His voice was quiet, but Stephanie leaned close.

"Stop this, Jeffery!" Stephanie demanded as she wiped back tears, "You will tell them yourself, both of them..."

Jeffery touched Stephanie's stomach and smiled.

"...Can I talk to Ariana?" Jeffery asked.

"Of course, you can. Wait just a minute. Mom!" Stephanie called out into the waiting room.

"Yes hun? How is he?" Stephanie's mom, Louise asked.

"I do not want to talk about that now. Can you send Ariana to me?" Stephanie responded with an edge in her voice.

"Where are we going mommy?" Ariana asked.

"We are going to see daddy." Stephanie replied.

"Yay I love my daddy." Ariana said excitedly.

"And he loves you too sweetheart." Stephanie responded.

"Hey, my two favorite ladies!" Jeffery said as Stephanie and Ariana walked into the room.

"Hi daddy." Ariana responded.

"So how is my little baby girl?" Jeffery asked.

"Good, but you sound bad daddy."

"It's okay, daddy has some things to tell you." Jeffery responded.

Stephanie looked away as she held back tears. Her heart crumbled; she wasn't ready to say goodbye to her hunni bunni, her stud muffin, her Prince Jeffery, best love, and father of her children.

"I cannot hear you so good daddy." Ariana responded.

"Daddy said that he has some things to tell you." Stephanie told Ariana.

"Thank you, mommy. I am listen to daddy." Ariana spoke as a three-year-old may.

Jeffery cleared his throat and spoke with all the strength he had left, "So, Ariana!" Jeffery continued.

"Yes daddy?" Ariana answered.

With a feeble voice Jeffery said, "Daddy loves you very much. I do not want you to ever forget that. I want you to always listen to your mother..." Jeffery delivered his first command.

"What about listening to you daddy?" Ariana asked. "You do not look good daddy. Are you sick?"

"You always listen to me." Jeffery smiled. "Please know that I will always be thinking of you, even if daddy is taking a real long nap and you cannot talk to him. You are so special and beautiful and wonderful. You're all things good. If anyone ever calls you ugly you tell them

17

you're beautiful because your daddy said so. No matter where you are in life, I will always be right there..." Jeffery continued offering the words he knew his sweet Ariana needed to hear. "Oh, and my little sweetheart..."

"What dad?" Ariana asked as she interrupted.

"Nothing, your mom will explain it one day." Jeffery answered.

"Why won't you explain it daddy?" Ariana asked with sadness in her voice.

"Because daddy is getting tired, and he will be sleeping." Jeffery answered.

"Okay daddy." Ariana provided a generic response as she was too young to fully comprehend all she had heard.

"Hey sweetheart I am going to talk to your mother, so I need you to go with mommy back to grandma. Hey, do not ever forget that daddy loves you the mostest." For the final time, Jeffery said the words Ariana loved to hear.

"No, I love you even more than the mostest." Ariana said as she gripped Stephanie's hand while walking away.

Tears fell from Jeffery's eyes. He wanted to stay with his family, make more memories, and watch Ariana grow up. He wanted to meet his unborn child. It pained him to know he would never watch Ariana get on the bus, glow in her prom dress or strut down the aisle as the most beautiful daughter. He tried reciting the serenity prayer, but tears overshadowed.

Stephanie walked slowly and ambivalently back towards the room. "Jeffery what are you saying?" Stephanie asked sadly when she returned to Jeffery's side.

"Stephanie you've been my rock, my best friend, and my sweetest sweetheart. I've loved you for as long as I could remember. We were childhood friends turned adult lovers and much more than our tiny sand-filled hands ever imagined..."

"Ha! We did go from playing together in the sandbox to holding hands just as close as we held our hearts. But Jeffery..."

"Don't Stephanie, you've got to let me go. There's nothing anyone else can do..."

Stephanie kissed Jeffery's lips, started to cry then began exiting the room. She quickly walked back to his side, sat, laid her head on his chest. She heeded every heartbeat, tears soiling his shirt, she whispered, "I love you."

"Mom!" Ariana called out, thus interrupting Stephanie's reverie.

"Yes hun?" Stephanie answered.

"Go! Go! Go! We gotta go." Ariana said enthusiastically.

"Is it time for the lesson?" Stephanie asked.

"Yes!" Ariana tugged on Stephanie's arm.

"Okay sweetie let me grab my purse." Stephanie said.

"What were you thinking about mommy?"

"Just life sweetie-that's all!"

"I don't know what that means." Ariana said as she tilted her head and looked bewilderingly at Stephanie.

"Get your shoes on please!" Stephanie prompted Ariana.

Stephanie and Ariana walked out of the door and towards the car. "How about we play your favorite CD in the car?" Stephanie said as she briefly rubbed Ariana's back.

The ride was solemnly sweet. Stephanie could not stop thinking about Jeffery. She and Ariana arrived at Harvey's studio five minutes early.

"Now five minutes early is more like it ladies." Harvey said jokingly.

"What? Don't you like a little extra time with us?" Stephanie chuckled flirtatiously.

"Oh, c'mon now, of course I do. Who wouldn't?" Harvey returned the subtle flirting.

Ariana smiled, "You're a nice man Harvey!"

Harvey smiled, "Well thank you very much. You're a nice little girl and a wonderful pianist for being so young."

"Okay you better get going Harvey. You do not want a repeat from last week!" Stephanie attempted to thwart Ariana's demands to promptly begin her lesson.

Harvey quickly complied, "Oh yeah, right! So why don't we start with your scales Ariana? I will play them one time, then it will be your turn."

Harvey played the scales, then Ariana did the same.

"Good job Ariana. Now let's make sure you understand which notes you're playing." Harvey said.

Harvey would point to a key and Ariana would name the note. After testing Ariana, he discovered that she knew approximately 80% of the notes on the piano. "Not bad Ariana! We have a little work to do, but you'll learn quickly."

"Good!" Ariana smiled.

Stephanie clapped. "You're awesome sweetie." Stephanie proclaimed.

Ariana's smiled enlarged, "Thank you mommy."

"I can't take it..." Harvey smirked, "You ladies are just too adorable."

"Heyyyyy, I'm not a lady...I'm a kid, a little girl ya know!"

Everyone laughed, first Harvey, followed quickly by Stephanie. Though confused, Ariana figured she should join in the laughter.

Stephanie smiled as she tucked her hair behind her right ear.

Harvey went through the keys and named each note for Ariana. He then gave her a sheet of paper highlighting and naming all notes on the piano.

"Okay Ariana let's run the scales once more then see how well you identify notes this time."

She did as Harvey instructed.

"Not bad at all Ariana. I want you to watch closely while I demonstrate appropriate fingering for you."

Harvey finished his demonstration. "We'll have to conclude soon, but does anyone have any questions?"

"I do!" Ariana raised her hand.

"You do not have to raise your hand Ariana, but I do appreciate you being such a respectful little girl." Harvey said.

"Ohhhh, thought I was a lady." Ariana inserted her charming sarcasm.

Stephanie shook her head in slight disbelief.

"Yeah, but..." Harvey began.

"Harvey do not..." Stephanie began overlapping Harvey.

"Okay, so Harvey?" Ariana interrupted. Stephanie threw her hands up in surrender.

"Yes?" Harvey answered.

"Why are you smiling?" Ariana asked an unexpected and difficult question.

Harvey looked at Stephanie, then back at Ariana, "What are you talking about?" He asked.

"You smile a lot." Ariana said.

"I smile because I am a happy person."

"Hmm, okay..." Ariana played a few notes on the piano.

Stephanie and Harvey traded stares and shared an awkward silence as the sound of Ariana's E-note faded.

Stephanie laughed, "Oh my, I think it may be time to go."

"I think you may be right Stephanie." Harvey agreed.

"Mommy, why does Mr. Harvey smile so much?"

"My sweet child, I do not know." Stephanie spoke quickly.

They finished the small talk and departed.

Now at home, Stephanie thought about Harvey, and it appeared that Ariana knew something she did not-That Harvey had a thing for her. "I'm not sure I can totally go for the dorky, nice guy type! He's cute though. No, he's handsome. And well the 'nice-guy type' can't be so bad after all." Stephanie reasoned.

Harvey was five feet nine inches tall. He was of a medium build, lacked muscle mass. He was slightly nerdy but had the face of an angel. Some would say he could have auditioned to be in a boyband and landed the part. His smile was infectious, and he had the kind of lips a girl would look forward to kissing. He wasn't much in the 'body' department, but Stephanie could tell that he was sweet at heart and worth exploring.

Though curious about Harvey, her heart yearned for Jeffery. It seemed like only yesterday he dipped her, kissed her and told her, *"Baby you are none short of the best part of my day."*

"You look lost a lot mommy." Ariana inched closer to her mother's leg.

"I do sweetie." Stephanie readily agreed.

"It's okay mommy." Ariana attached herself to her mother's leg.

"Hey Ariana, it's time for dinner. You and Johnny will be eating all your vegetables tonight." Stephanie informed Ariana.

Ariana rolled her eyes, "But mom, Johnathan is only two and I am only five." Ariana replied.

"Oh yeah you're right." Stephanie nudged Ariana and smiled. She was fond of Ariana's ability to advocate for herself and others as well as negotiate for what she wanted. "And you're still eating your vegetables so you can grow up big and strong."

Ariana perked up, "I'm strong enough."

"What about getting bigger?"

"Ummm..." Ariana's quick wit failed her.

"Ahh gotcha, now go get your brother."

"Fine, you win...this time!"

CHAPTER 4

They ate as a family at the dining room table, though the family felt incomplete. Two years had passed since Jeffery's death and dinner time was hardest for Stephanie. She'd always wanted to have a family that spent quality time together, and that included eating together at the dinner table.

Johnathan would never come to know his father and the amazing man he was. Ariana's memories would be few and would eventually fade. Stephanie's memories went back to the day they found each other once again.

Jeffery walked into Stephanie's job, dressed to the nines and sporting a captivating, gentle smile. He was traveling to market his new technological invention: a cell phone application of some sort. He laid eyes on Stephanie, rendered speechless, Jeffery marveled at her meticulous attention to detail as he watched her work.

It was love at first sight as though they were meeting for the first time. A few moments escaped, yet for Jeffery time stood still until Stephanie slowly raised her eyes. Flipping her hair behind her ear, she smiled. It was at that moment Jeffery became certain she would fall for him as he knew he had fallen for her.

"Hey aren't you..."
"Jeffery, and you are not the kind of lady I could ever forget."
"Yeah, quite the impression I suppose."

They shared the first laugh of many to come.

Stephanie was beautiful, sophisticated, and her eyes would put any man under whatever spell she wanted. And Jeffery was under her spell! He was well-dressed and walked with an aura of confidence. Stephanie was captivated.
Somehow, they knew they would fall in love. And they did. Smiles were many and arguments few. Laughs were plenty and tears were mostly of joy. They were like two kids when they looked at each other and concerning intimacy: they were like two kids-only this time in a candy store. Everything looked good, smelled good, felt good and tasted good. They just couldn't get enough of each other.
They held hands and looked toward Heaven after one romantic evening. The

moon and stars smiled in approval of what had been created...Love between two people meant to be. Their lives and their love moved quickly, they kept the pace, faith and stayed the course. They were a match made in Heaven.

Jeffery was the type of guy her mom knew she would marry-adventurous, successful, and chivalrous. For the first time Stephanie truly loved a man. So many men had used her, taken what they wanted and left her to clean up the mess. She maintained virtue.

She was scarred and bruised badly from past hurts. Somehow Jeffery made falling in love seem safe. He frequently told Stephanie, "If you fall, I will catch you and always love you the very best that I can. You will be number one and I will be number two because I want to put you first. You're the best thing that has ever happened to me."

Stephanie would smile at the sweet words of Jeffery because she knew he meant every word. With him she was safe. Her heart jumped for joy at the thought of Jeffery and the future she could have with him. Then one day it happened. In the middle of a 4th of July parade he went down on one knee. Sparks were already flying, literally-so he figured why not add to the fireworks. Well not to the surprise of anyone- she said yes. They planned a wedding with the help of Stephanie's friend who was a wedding coordinator. Jeffery stood at the altar waiting for the woman he called his 'best choice.' Then she walked through the doors and Jeffery's eyes couldn't take it any longer. He cried at the transition his life was making and who he was writing life's next chapter with. Tears of joy streamed his face. Stephanie was what and who he wanted. He was her present and her future and that is what mattered.

They stood together at the altar holding hands and sharing the depth of what was in their hearts. Finally, the moment came when they delivered the words which began a new chapter in their lives- "I do!" Just like that, they became one. They were now a 'we' and no longer an 'I'. He changed her last name, and she changed his life.

A couple of years went by, and they were expecting their first child. Jeffery and Stephanie survived the first couple of years of marriage. In all fairness to the term, they thrived. They were fully committed to forever and Jeffery never missed a beat. With each new sunrise, He loved her more than the day before. Their eyes still burned for each other as much as it did that day at Stephanie's job. The moon and stars smiled.

No one knows in advance the day of their demise, so Stephanie and Jeffery adopted a *carpe diem* philosophy. Eventually Stephanie conquered the pain of her past. One ex-boyfriend was physically and verbally abusive. Another ex-boyfriend was a chronic cheater, and consequently most cheaters surface as liars. Worst of all was when she broke up with an ex that didn't like her leaving him, he threatened her life if she didn't abort their unborn child. Well, Stephanie was no pushover, but his hard punch to the stomach terminated the life growing inside her. For her unborn child, the day of demise came before the first daybreak. Stephanie's child would never have a name, never take a breath outside of the womb, never experience growing up, compounding this tragedy-her child would never receive a proper burial. She would never see the child's face, hold the child close, and Stephanie would never know what it would be like to watch her first child grow up. Stephanie learned that authentic love could heal wounds.

Stephanie did not think she would ever recover from her violent and involuntary abortion, but Jeffery helped her look forward to new memories. She suppressed what she could. Jeffery reminded her of the well-known adage, "Yesterday is history, tomorrow is a mystery and today is a gift!" Jeffery encouraged Stephanie to memorialize her past, look forward to tomorrow and make the most unforgettable memories in the day that she'd been blessed with- 'Today!'

Stephanie and Jeffery made many remarkable memories. They skydived and rode the Jet Ski. They had romantic dinners and enjoyed countless comedy shows. They played chess, and checkers, and arm wrestled for fun. With groups of friends, they enjoyed hiking, sporting events and games like Apples to Apples, Monopoly, and many others. They danced like kids who had eaten too much candy, and most of all they laughed. Then they brought a beautiful little girl into the world. They called her name Ariana, and their love grew because of the life they were now jointly responsible for loving, nurturing, and keeping safe.

Stephanie did not like that Jeffery was a procrastinator; he was an amazing man, nonetheless. Stephanie complained quite a bit around the house, but Jeffery loved her more than words could express. Periodically they had healthy arguments that healthy couples typically had. Length of time away from the house, what it meant to be a family, child rearing and the like. Stephanie did not like Jeffery using tobacco, but he could not break the habit. They were raised slightly differently in

31

terms of discipline. Jeffery supported spanking, but Stephanie did not. Jeffery was also in agreement with time-out but was totally hands-on. Stephanie thought he needed to relax a little. Ariana was so little that there was minimal need for discipline. Capitalizing on teachable moments was more of what usually took place.

Regardless of the quarrel or qualm, Stephanie and Jeffery were two peas in a pod. They were elated adding a third pea to the pod-Ariana. They found joy in the smallest of milestones and achievements: Ariana's first word, her first step and her smiling at them. Watching her develop and grow was more special than Stephanie or Jeffery ever thought possible. Indeed, she had a way of bringing much more joy to their hearts.

Jeffery melted like ice cream in the presence of his baby girl. She was an extension of her mother which made loving her even sweeter. He would give his life for her without a second thought. When holding her for the first time, he experienced a feeling like never before-unconditional love and surrender to whatever would make his little Ariana smile. Without question he knew he was meant to love her unconditionally forever. Stephanie admired the way Jeffery looked at Ariana. She knew he would be a great father. She smiled at the way her life had come together. She could ask for nothing more. Jeffery was amazing beyond belief and Ariana was sweeter than apple pie.

They walked through life together, side-by-side, day-by-day. One moment at a time they conquered life as one. She loved him more than she thought possible. Every girl wants to be a princess, and Jeffery offered her that opportunity. He was the kind of man that made a woman want to be better. He would say the same about her. It was simply a relationship that worked. She was his "Princess Stephanie" and he was her "Prince Jeffery."

Her memories momentarily concluded, and the family finished their meal then Stephanie got the children ready for bed.

"Have sweet dreams mommy, I love you." Ariana said sweetly as she planted a kiss on her mother's cheek.

Two-year-old Johnathan just smiled and said whatever words he had learned at his young age.

Stephanie sat on the couch after a long and draining day, she couldn't believe she was a widowed, single mother at the age of 30. She wanted to cry herself to sleep, but her mother had always taught to be strong.

CHAPTER 5

There is a preface to every story.

Harvey wasn't much of a serial dater. He'd had a couple of girlfriends, but Harvey's primary focus was his career as an accomplished pianist and instructor.

Harvey was 26 years of age and he'd fallen head over heels for the 'perfect girl', Andrea - at least in his opinion she was perfect. She played piano as well, she was funny, outgoing, and strikingly beautiful! She was sensual, sexual and had moves like an exotic dancer - the complete package some would say. She loved and enjoyed life to the best of her ability. She made sure to spend time with friends, to spend time playing piano, going to the movies, spending time with family, hanging out with Harvey, and occasionally going out for a night on the town.

"Hey babe..." Andrea greeted with excitement.

Harvey was tired from the night before, so he answered the phone very groggily, He-hel-hello..."

"Babe, I have great news!" Andrea said with immense excitement.

"Not just good, but great? I love great news so let me hear it dear." Harvey responded.

"I am pregnant."

Harvey smiled a little. He always wanted to be a father, but he never really liked surprises. "Uh...that's great dear, it really is." Harvey responded with unsteadiness in his voice.

At this point Harvey and Andrea had been dating exclusively for a little more than a year. Harvey did not detect any real problems regarding the relationship. He needed to ask certain pertinent and preliminary questions, but ultimately, he was excited.

"Oh my, are you sure?" Harvey asked.

"Yes, silly, I am sure. Two pregnancy tests have come back positive, and I have an appointment with my doctor tomorrow." Andrea answered rather candidly.

"Okay babe well it looks like we have some planning to do." Harvey demonstrated his readiness to join her in the next phase of their lives.

"Yes, we do handsome." Andrea replied.

"Wait!" Harvey's curiosity began settling.

"What babe?" Andrea answered.

"You're sure the child is mine?"

"Why would you even ask me such a ridiculous question? Of course, the child is yours. I would never cheat on you. I love you!" Andrea answered Harvey's question with unwavering confidence.

"I know dear, I know." Harvey passively responded. Though insecure, Harvey loved Andrea deeply and worked hard to believe she would not disrespect the love they shared.

Harvey went to the doctor's appointment with Andrea, and she was right-she was expecting. The look on Harvey's face revealed precisely the kind of father he intended to be. Harvey smiled wide. He hugged Andrea tightly. They kissed, the passion and joy were apparent. The ambiguity present upon finding out Andrea was pregnant gradually lessened as she continued reassuring Harvey. Harvey took his insecurities, packed them neatly into a mental box and buried them in a safe place-A safe place which could lead to detrimental actions if endangered.

Harvey was involved in all the pre-birth activities. He made late night runs for Andrea's weird food cravings: pickles and ice cream, potato chips and frosting, sweet tea and whipped cream. Harvey often made the joke that his attorney would be sending her a bill for food and gas. They laughed often, but Andrea seemed aloof at times. Harvey didn't know if it was simply a part of the hormonal happenings associated with pregnancy, or if something was wrong on a deeper level. Only Andrea could answer the question of whether her mood was affected by something besides being pregnant. Andrea admitted periodic frustration with Harvey's imbalanced mood and problems trusting her.

They made it through the pregnancy all right and the day came to welcome their little girl into the world. They named her Raina Ari. She was the most beautiful little girl. Harvey was the second person to hold Raina, after Andrea of course. The moment was special and fitting for candid camera as well as a high costing hallmark card. Harvey held Raina close to his chest, a tear fell. He'd rank holding Raina for the first time as the greatest moment of his life.

Though enjoying fatherhood, Harvey's paranoia had not dissipated. He loved Raina more than he believed he could ever love anyone. When she looked at him with her beautiful, bright blue eyes Harvey was instantly caught in her spell. He would give his life for hers, and likewise he'd take a life to save hers. Harvey finally experienced authentic, sacrificial, and unconditional love. Raina loved her daddy. She smiled whenever he was near. Andrea was equally loving, engaging and involved as a mother. They were a cohesive and happy family.

All that Harvey wanted to do was be an amazing boyfriend and father. He planned to propose but did not feel certain it was the right thing to do.

Once again, he could tell that something was troubling Andrea. "Baby what's wrong?" He would often ask.

"Nothing handsome!" Was Andrea's typical response.

Harvey would grab Andrea, square their shoulders, look right at her, and say, "Please know that you can talk to me about anything beautiful."

"I know I can Harvey, you're the sweetest boyfriend ever." Andrea would often respond.

"But why does it feel like sometimes you are a million miles away." This thought was usually in response to what Harvey believed to be Andrea's superficial pre-rehearsed response.

"Andrea..." Harvey called out once after hearing the generic response, one time too many.

"What?" Andrea answered.

"When I look into your eyes, I do not see you."

"Baby what do you mean?" Andrea asked, attempting to soothe her need for clarification.

"You seem to be a million miles away. I just wish you'd talk to me." Harvey responded with a sense of desperation defining his voice.

Andrea lowered her eyes, then looked back up, "I'm fine!" Andrea responded with fabricated emotion.

"No, you're not. Why are you shutting me out? We used to actually talk..." Harvey paused... "Openly and honestly!" He continued. Harvey was visibly frustrated. He loved Andrea and truly wanted to make her happy.

"I have to give Raina a bath now." Andrea walked away. "I should just tell him. He loves me and he will understand." She thought as she walked slowly towards Raina's crib.

Harvey knew that something was wrong, but rather than expend energy figuring out what has been troubling Andrea he decided to focus on his relationship with Raina.

The next several months passed without many changes in the relationship between Harvey and Andrea. Raina felt loved. Harvey could not say the same for himself. He felt loved, admired, and needed by Raina, but did not feel the same from Andrea.

Raina Ari's first birthday party was great. On the surface was a united family, a child loved by many, and two families well-blended. Harvey and Andrea's families occasionally had joint family nights, shared birthday parties, and periodically engaged in fun activities such as bowling, trampoline parks and so on.

Raina wanted her daddy more than anyone, and without limit or question he obliged.

During the next year Raina Ari continued growing, learning new language, and of course developing her personality. Andrea was relatively distant, but more present since Harvey told her, "When I look at you, I don't see you." Whatever she wrestled with remained her most debilitating secret. She observed the way Harvey and Raina's relationship developed with such wonder and grace. She admired Harvey's relationship with Raina and its natural, remarkable progression. Deep inside Andrea knew it was time for a long-awaited conversation with Harvey.

Harvey and Raina were lying watching "Inside Out". It was Raina's favorite movie. Andrea interrupted as she called out from their bedroom, "Harvey..."

Harvey turned to look.

"We need to talk..." Andrea responded.

CHAPTER 6

Remembering brought Harvey pain so he decided it was time to get up and go about his day. Harvey looked at his daily planner and realized he had forgotten something important, "Oh no today is the annual cookout for my students!" He said aloud.

Harvey jumped up, got ready for the day then checked the RSVP list. "I wonder if I should call Stephanie." Ariana was a new student, so Harvey was unsure if he informed had Stephanie of the annual cookout.

Stephanie was getting ready to take the kids to the park when her phone began to ring. "Why is Harvey calling me? I know Ariana's lesson is not until Tuesday, it's only Saturday. Hmm maybe Ariana was right about Harvey and the way he looks at me, "Hello!" She ended her haste rationalization.

"Hi Stephanie, sorry to bother you on this Saturday morning..." Harvey began immediately after Stephanie answered. He had no clue about Stephanie's schedule but did hope to chat momentarily.

"It's okay Harvey, to what do I owe this call?" Stephanie tried to be patient, but really wanted to resume her morning tasks.

"Well, every year I do an annual cookout for my students and with Ariana being new I think I forgot to invite you all." Stephanie couldn't see the way Harvey's cheek bones and slight squinting revealed that he really wanted her to come.

"Geez thanks Harvey, I see how important we are to you!" Stephanie teased.

"I am really sorry Stephanie. I totally suck!" Harvey pressed his right index finger into his temple and rubbed about. He did not like to inconvenience others, yet being an only child caused him to justify this action at times-particularly when reveling in his glorious sense of entitlement.

"Uh Harvey I am just joking." Stephanie said with a slightly higher pitch than her previous statement. Harvey had yet to learn Stephanie's style of communication, and the significant role that sarcasm played.

Laughing, Harvey responded, "Oh whew, good!" It wasn't hard for Stephanie to quickly figure out how credulous Harvey was. This made teasing him more exciting and adventurous.

After a brief silence Harvey asked, "So can you guys come? It will be from 3:00 PM to 7:00 PM." Harvey tilted his head slightly to the left and touched his side.

"Well let me run my daily list in my head..." Stephanie took a moment to make a mental note of her errands and engagements for the day. "Um okay we will see you at 3:00."

Since Jeffery's death Stephanie had been a single mother of two young children. She had come to accept that being a busy single mother may be the cards of life she would have to play.

"That is awesome, I look forward to seeing you guys." Harvey said with exuberance.

"Oh, hey Harvey?" Stephanie called out.

"Yes?" Harvey replied. Harvey was particularly interested in what Stephanie had to say.

"Where are you having the cookout? Should I bring a dish to pass or anything else?" Her voice was mild and aloof, showing only minimal interest in the details yet fully aware of interest in her.

"It will just be in my backyard, and just bring yourselves." Harvey answered stoically in response to Stephanie's ostensible lack of interest.

"Okay then I will see you at 3:00 PM." Stephanie informed Harvey. Harvey could not see it, but Stephanie wore a light smile. She reached for her candy apple red lipstick - her favorite. She ran her fingers through her long blonde hair. She smiled once more.

"See you then." Harvey hung up quickly. He grabbed his pen and added Stephanie and Ariana name as confirmed guests. It was the first time in 3 years he longed for anyone as much as he did Andrea.

One thing about Harvey is that he had always been very organized. Even as a young child he kept his toys and shoes more organized than most boys his age. His organizational skills aided him when preparing for the cookout.

Harvey went to the store to pick up a few items more for the cookout. There would be grilled hot dogs, chicken and burgers, condiments and macaroni salad with potato chips and soft beverages. Harvey was not a man fond of alcohol consumption. From a very young age he developed indifference for drinking alcohol because of how he interpreted the bible. Most people that heard of this anomalous character trait presumed Harvey was from a family which battled the demons of alcoholism-A theoretical hypothesis further from the truth than if you'd called

Harvey President of the United States of America. Harvey simply liked the notion of being unique.

Harvey spent the morning and part of the afternoon behind the grill and preparing the tables. Now it was almost 2:00 and Harvey was in a major race against the clock. Harvey had few friends and was often reclusive.

"Is there anything we can help with Mr. Harvey?" The earlier than expected guest (s) asked. Harvey clasped his hands and smiled. He took a deep breath to mentally adjust to their unexpected arrival. Harvey identified with the Type-A personality. He was a man of order, and guests arriving reeked of disorder.

Harvey turned around, showing the grill his back! He was surprised to see Ariana and her younger brother, Johnathan standing there. Then Harvey looked up and was undeniably mesmerized by Stephanie's smile. "Hello Harvey." She knew exactly how to woo and wow a man. Her candy apple red lipstick glistened with a hint of silver metallic sparkles. Her skirt was fitted, but completely fitting for a lady - the skirt reached to her knees. Because she would be outdoors, she wore a pair of flats that somehow complimented her black skirt as well as her silver Chanel top which covered her butt. Her earrings were diamond studded with a silver half-hoop, which eloquently complimented her outfit-especially the lavish Chanel top.

"Hello there Stephanie." Harvey smiled back, "Thank you so much for coming to help. That was very nice of you." Her beauty was inspiring and invoking, "Oh my, oh my, you are super cute..." Harvey offered a passive compliment as he scratched the inside of his right shorts pocket.

Stephanie stared as if to communicate that Harvey needed to improve upon his ability to give adequate compliments.

Harvey allowed his arms to fall limp by either side of his body, "I meant to say that you look absolutely gorgeous!" He began shaking his head from side to side, presuming another failed attempt had transpired.

"That is better!" Stephanie smiled and pointed her right index finger at him.

Harvey smiled and crossed one foot in front of the other. He turned around and reached for the tongs to the grill, but quickly turned back to face Stephanie.

"We weren't doing much around the house so we decided to come and see if the 'one-man-show' could use some help." Stephanie barreled in laughter.

"Well, I could definitely use your help, so thank you!" Harvey clasped his hands together and bowed his head a bit. "Oh, and I am glad you know how to make yourself laugh, it's adorable!"

"You're welcome and thank you!" Stephanie smiled. "What can we do to help?" She asked as she inched slightly closer to Harvey.

"You guys can set the tables. The condiments are right over there in the garage." Harvey replied quickly as he hurried about. "Sorry, I hope I am not being rude. I just feel like I, well, we are in a grueling race against the clock."

Stephanie smiled and moved towards the napkins sitting by the grill, "It's okay, you're simply a man of order." Stephanie grabbed the napkins then noticed condiments on the opposite side of the grill. "We are on it, Mr. Harvey!" Stephanie said jokingly.

"Hey, I'm counting on ya." Harvey winked.

Harvey watched as Stephanie walked away. "She sure is beautiful. I'm glad I mustered the confidence to tell her earlier. Bold move, bold move!" Harvey said of him complimenting a woman he barely knew.

Ariana hurried over to Harvey to tell him of her observation, "I see you looking at my mom." Ariana informed Harvey smiled a little as she bounced up and down.

"No, you don't!" Harvey attempted to tickle Ariana.

From a distance Stephanie looked in awe, "Wow no man has been this good with her since her dad." Stephanie stopped and scratched her head, in deep thought she said, "Never mind, it will never happen...just forget it, Stephanie!" Tears began to form in her eyes as she was moved by the interaction between Harvey and Ariana.

Stephanie pinched herself to see if this feeling was real. She was starting to think of Harvey in ways she did not think she would. She was starting to feel things that she had no intentions of feeling. Despite efforts she was unable to deny that something was beginning to grow inside of her.

"Stephanie?" Harvey called out.
"Yes Harvey?" Her smile communicated she'd been having

thoughts other than preparing for the party.

"I just wanted to say thank you so much for coming early to help me out. It was really nice of you and honestly..." Harvey paused.

"Honestly what?" Stephanie asked immediately after crossing her arms.

"Are you always this defensive?" Harvey communicated his stark disapproval of Stephanie's response.

"I'm sorry. I'm not usually like this."

"Well, are you alright?" Harvey asked as unfolded his arms and put his hands in pockets. Harvey felt mildly frustrated that he'd confronted Stephanie so soon.

"I'm fine. What were you going to say?" Stephanie asked in a more appropriate and non-defensive tone of voice.

During the silence Stephanie thought, "Gosh and he is genuinely nice." She ran both index fingers through either side of her hair.

Harvey was totally smitten by Stephanie's beauty, "I was just going to say it has been nice spending time with you outside of the lessons and also I..." Harvey began, but was, per se, unexpectedly interrupted.

"What are you guys talking about?" Ariana interjected.

"Hey what did I tell you about interrupting adults when they are talking?" Stephanie said firmly as she shot Ariana a serious look.

"I'm sorry mommy." Ariana readily apologized.

"Go play please." Her tone was dark and hard.

Ariana ran away and began to play with Johnathan.

"Whoa you are pretty strict I see!" Harvey laughed.

"I suppose I am a little strict." Stephanie smiled as she rolled her eyes sarcastically. "What were you going to say Harvey?"

"Nothing!" Harvey returned the smile.

"Oh, c'mon you gotta tell me now." Stephanie showed Harvey her puppy dog eyes.

"I was just wondering where Ariana's father is at." Harvey quickly replied.

Stephanie looked down then back up with heavier eyes, and not so puppy dog-like, "I do not want to talk about that!" Stephanie said quickly and with a hint of harsh.

"I am sorry. I did not mean to open a wound or anything..." Harvey was quick to amend his offence. His right hand tapped, off rhythm nonetheless, the inside of his short pocket. Harvey wasn't dressed as stunningly as Stephanie. He sported tan cargo shorts and a black t-shirt with black sneakers to match.

"It's okay, you couldn't have known." Stephanie responded with a tone that was easy on the ears-much less harsh than the tone she had previously used.

The silence reassured Harvey that something was wrong.

"Well, we should get ready to greet all the guests." Harvey quickly transitioned, with hopes of abandoning the prior conversation.

"We?" Stephanie responded with curiosity. She smiled as she tilted her head slightly.

"Uh yes, we! Come on." Harvey grabbed Stephanie's arm and ran playfully towards the back door.

Stephanie wasn't sure how she felt about Harvey touching her, but she went with it. She assumed he was well-intentioned and playful by nature.

The guests filed in, and the cookout started off well. The students enjoyed getting to know each other, and the parents enjoyed the intermingling just the same. Harvey was happy with the little bit of progress he had made with Stephanie. He figured he'd know the right moment to make a more definitive move.

A sullen mood came over Harvey and he had no clue as to why. As cleanup was being completed it all made sense to Harvey. He said his goodbyes but saved the best for last. He lightly hugged Stephanie; the smell of her perfume was sweet yet savory. Their eyes met, "I am looking forward to Ariana's lesson!" Harvey smiled. He interlocked his hands then bit his bottom lip.

There was something about the look in their eyes that mesmerized the other. Neither was sure how or when, but their eyes told a tale of love to come. The end remained a mystery, but the beginning appeared pre-determined.

"Oh look!" Harvey told Stephanie, "There's Andrea. She's here to drop off Raina; my god-daughter."
"I am looking forward to meeting her." Stephanie replied.

Harvey walked towards the sidewalk to greet Andrea and Raina.

"Thank you for dropping her off."
Harvey hugged Andrea. Their embrace
warmed Harvey's heart and caused him to
momentarily miss her touch.

"You're welcome. Have a good day
baby." Andrea told Raina. "Take care of
yourself Harvey and thank you for
continuing to spend time with Raina. She
loves you."

Harvey smiled. "Hey Raina, I want
you to meet Stephanie, Johnathan and
Ariana." He said as the 3 of them walked
toward the front of yard. Pleasantries were
exchanged. "Do you kids want to play in
the sandbox?" Harvey asked. Almost
simultaneously Raina, Ariana and
Johnathan yelled out, "yeah!"

Stephanie and Harvey sat on the
bench, soaking the sun and marveling at
the care-free play. Harvey was reminded of
a moment of his own childhood. Harvey
was awakened in the middle of the night.
He was home alone with his mother.

"What are you doing mom?" Harvey
asked.
"Shhh, just follow me." His mother
responded.

They walked at a medium pace from
Harvey's bedroom to the first floor then

into the basement. As a 6-year-old Harvey trusted his parents with his life. He had no reason to suspect his mother to be anything except good to him.

"Why are we in the basement?" Harvey asked. "Where is dad?"

"Your father is at work." His mother said while hitting Harvey in the head."

His mother quickly sat him down and tied him to a chair. He regained consciousness after approximately 48 seconds. His immediate reaction was normal and to be expected.

"Mom!" Harvey yelled as loud as he could as a 6-year-old boy.

His mother paced back and forth. "We have work to do Harvey. Evil is suppressed deep within you."

"Mom please untie me." Harvey cried profusely.

"Not until..."

"I want dad. I want dad now."

"The only person that can help you now is the God almighty." His mother responded.

Harvey did what he had heard his parents often do. He prayed, "God please. Please God, I need..."

Harvey's mother covered his mouth. She looked at Harvey. A look and a moment Harvey would never forget. "I will pray, you will listen."

Because Harvey respected his parents, he stopped praying.

"God, we know evil is real because you created it; You and you, alone. Therefore God, you and you alone can remove the evil that lives and lurks inside of my son. Dear God, I pray that you make him holy. Keep his mind pure. God protect him from those demons lurking the earth."

His mother began to walk around Harvey. She periodically sprinkled olive oil on his head. "One day God, one day this little boy will..."

Confused and afraid, Harvey whimpered. He had to do something. He squirmed, but to no avail. "Mom!" He yelled.

"Harvey! Harvey!" Stephanie called out as she shook Harvey.

"Hey, yeah, what is it Stephanie?" Harvey said as he shook his head from side to side.

"Are you okay?" Stephanie asked.

"I am great, why?" Harvey smiled as he asked.

"I think you were...never mind."

For a moment neither Stephanie nor Harvey spoke.

"I am too. I'm looking forward to the lesson also." Stephanie responded. She hid the emotion behind her words somewhat better than Harvey. With both hands behind her back, Stephanie rubbed her thumbs inconspicuously across one another. Ariana noticed this exchange of behavior between her mom and Mr. Harvey.

"Um it's my lesson, what about me?" Ariana chimed in. For being a five-year-old girl speaking to her mother, she was a little too sassy.

Johnathan smiled; his language was still relatively undeveloped.

Harvey kneeled, "Well of course I am looking forward to your lesson and hearing how awesomely you play once again." Harvey reassured Ariana.

Ariana smiled, "Thank you Mr. Harvey!"

Harvey couldn't take his eyes off Ariana. "Harvey why are you staring at me?"

"...I'm sorry it's just that, you really remind me of another little girl that's pretty awesome just like you." Harvey explained his constant stares. His eyes glistened, but only he could fully understand the smile that he wore.

CHAPTER 7

That night Harvey tossed and turned as he struggled to sleep. His internal anguish was just that-internal. He remembered like it was yesterday, "Harvey we need to talk..." Those were the words spoken by Andrea, the love of his life. Andrea was ready to reveal the secret that held her heart and emotions hostage for more than five years.

"Anything baby!" Harvey said. His voice though mild, embodied a hint of curiosity.

"Raina, can you go to your room for a moment?" Andrea asked as she moved her long hair from beside her face to behind her ear. She looked as a woman already defeated-her lips just about scowled.

"Sure mommy." Raina spoke calmly. Raina was usually a very respectful child and did not fuss when her mother or father asked her to do something.

"Okay baby what did you want to talk to me about?" Harvey's eyebrows raised a notch, and his eyes, though unassuming, enlarged depicting his profound interest and concern for the developing conversation.

"It's Raina Ari!" Andrea began. She held her head down and looked at the floor as she spoke her daughter's name.

"Okay, um what about her?" Harvey asked. His eyes grew larger, he crossed his arms and leaned in a little closer.

"She's not yours!" Andrea delivered the heartbreaking news. A tear began to form, one in each eye.

Harvey sat up on the couch, "Uh..." Harvey uncrossed his arms, then scratched his head. "...Is this a joke?" His eyes darkened and embodied a look of confusion.

"Baby I wish it was a joke. You're the greatest guy ever. You're the best father she could have asked for!" Andrea began to cry. She then gave in to the full spectrum of the emotional weight resting heavily upon her. Her legs gave way, her knees buckled...she collapsed.

"One really big problem- She's...Not...My..." Harvey stopped. He couldn't bear to say the words.

"It doesn't have to change anything baby." Andrea began to plead as she slid towards the edge of the plush blue couch where Andrea and Harvey had spent so much time learning, loving and now losing each other.

"You're sitting here, talking about nothing changing! You just changed everything!" Harvey yelled. He quickly rose to his feet.

"Please calm down Harvey!" Andrea's eyes foretold an anecdote of fear, worry and ambivalence.

"Don't tell me to calm down. You calm the..." Harvey paused, then began pacing around the living room. "How could you? How could you Andrea?" Harvey clenched his fists, then released all tension.

"Baby I am sorry. I made a huge mistake, but I have been faithful ever since." Andrea searched for approval, for belief and for forgiveness, but Harvey's eyes showed the thing Andrea hoped and prayed it would not-Disdain and no easy determiner of the next step.

"Mistake? Ha ha...A mistake is playing the wrong note. A mistake is selecting premium instead of regular gas. Cheating is just blatant disrespect. What happened?" The pupils had formed like a puppy looking for love to return.

"Well, I went..." Andrea began.

"You know what, I don't even want to know!" Harvey interrupted. He put his right hand on his forehead and shook his head from side to side.

"Harvey I am so sorry, but please I do not want us to change. We can still play piano together, dance around and be silly, take Raina to the park and for ice cream, we can make love and walk in love, 'we', 'this' does not have to change. Please do not let it change us babe. You're the best guy I've ever found!" Andrea had now risen to her feet and moved quickly to stand face to face with Harvey.

"Apparently not!" Harvey tried to be strong, but the waterworks in his eyes told the complete truth.

"Now what babe?" Andrea asked, hoping today wasn't the last of many memories and that she would not have to begin adjusting to life without the man of her dreams.

"I do not know. I need time to think. I am going to step out. I will call you." Harvey grabbed his baseball hat and began walking towards the door. He paused his steps and thought of turning around. Though he decided to continue walking.

"Daddy!" Raina Ari said as she ran towards the door. Her big blue eyes displayed pure, unadulterated love.

Harvey stopped in his tracks but couldn't bear to turn around. Raina hugged the back of his legs, "I love you daddy, don't leave-We have to finish watching our favorite movie." Raina said in the sweetest voice Harvey had ever heard as tears began to form. Leaving Andrea was god-awfully hard. Leaving Raina was devastating beyond repair.

Harvey did not want his little baby girl to see him crying, but he wasn't left much choice. Raina scaled his body with hers, gripped his legs and looked up at him, "Why are you sad daddy?" Raina's soft eyes and meek smile shattered Harvey's heart into a million pieces-He crumbled.

"Sweetie, daddy just has a lot to think about." Harvey held his left hand over his eyes while his right-hand gripped Raina's back. The touch was powerful.

"Well why don't you and mommy talk about it like you do all those other times?" Raina asked as her pupils enlarged.

"Because this is something daddy has to think about by himself." Harvey responded as best he knew how.

"That's no fun dad!" Raina said as her left hand moved to her hip.

"Raina, I will see you later okay. And if I do not then I promise to call." Harvey did the best he could to hide his tears from Raina.

"Will you be back daddy?" Raina asked with a hint of worry and sadness in her voice.

Andrea walked closer and grabbed Raina, "Raina come on, let him go." Andrea said as she choked back the tears she had been crying during this exchange.

Andrea hid her sadness as best as she could to avoid upsetting Raina. Though only three years old, Raina she knew that something was wrong.

"Hey dad?" Raina turned partially from her mother's grip.

"Yes sweetie?" Harvey attempted to hide the depth of what he was feeling inside.

"Love you to the sun..." Raina smiled as she awaited Harvey's response.

"Love you too my number one." Harvey laughed through the tears he choked back. He knew when he stepped out of the door, he would be walking away from so much he had come to love.

Harvey walked out of the front door at 8:23 PM on a Thursday night. He felt dejected, rejected and as though Andrea had ripped his world away from him. He sat on the park bench for hours trying to convince himself to go back. His sadness was overwhelming. "How could she betray me this way?" Harvey placed his elbows on his knees and held his head in his hands.

A part of him wished she'd never told him, but likewise part of him was glad that she did. He wondered why it took her three years as well as the length of time that she was pregnant. "I loved Raina with all of me. I gave the best of me, and this is how that...that woman repays me!" Harvey stood up and kicked at the park bench.

Harvey gazed into the night sky hoping for a sign, consolation of sorts, but the galaxy and the universe were quiet. His heart was broken and like the song reminded, "Mama said there'd be days like this. There'd be days like this my mama said!"

Upon checking his watch Harvey noticed that it was almost 1:00 AM. He'd sat on that bench thinking and sulking for more than four hours. His heart and mind discovered no comfortable place to meet. He knew he'd have no peace tonight and several nights to come. He wanted to return home but knew it would be too painful.

He was always welcomed at his parents' house. He gave them a courtesy call then went to stay there for a few days. He called Andrea and said, "I want to remain a part of Raina's life, but I am not so sure about us." Harvey remained relatively calm and nice for a man wrestling with such betrayal as Harvey was.

"I understand, and of course you can remain a part of Raina's life. I hope one day you can find it in your heart to

forgive me and give me a second chance."
From a heartfelt place Andrea spoke the
words she felt would never happen.

"Thank you. Can I see her this
weekend?" Harvey asked indifferently.

"Of course." Andrea said with a
slightly higher pitch voice and blatant joy
for Harvey seeing Raina. The covert reason
for her happiness was the opportunity to
spend time with Harvey again.

"Okay I will call you on Saturday."
The piano was nearby, but Harvey decided
this, "I have no interest right now." He
tapped his fingers as he contemplated his
most logical response to the situation.

"Harvey?" Andrea called out.

"What is it, Andrea?" Harvey
responded as he stared around the room
where he used to sleep. He and Andrea
used to play cards, eat food, play board
games, and do lots of other stuff in his
bedroom before they decided to move in
together.

With her hands-free cell phone
device in ear, Andrea laid both hands open
on the kitchen table, "I love you and I do
not like this. We do not have to let go of
what we have." Her voice trailed and
embodied sadness and hurt.

"I love you too Andrea. I really do,
but I need time." Harvey shook his head
from left to right, presumably from
frustration and disbelief.

"Okay well I will not pressure you."
Andrea responded in a tone indicative of
disappointment.

"Who was it? Who did you cheat on
me with?" Harvey asked in a very tight-
lipped manner.

"Harvey, you do not want to know
babe. Can we not have this conversation?"
Andrea said passively and a bit somberly.

The look on Harvey's face went from
mildly frustrated to visibly upset, "First of
all do not call me babe, second of all I do
want to know." Harvey leaned against his
bathroom wall. His voice merely direct. He
delivered the message harshly as he
tapped his right foot. His hands did not
know how to express what they were
feeling.

Andrea sat on her bed. She began
shaking her head, and tears began to
form. "Fine it was some guy I met at the
gym, Reynolds was the last name or
something like that!"

"How? When? You know what, never
mind! I knew that guy was no good."

"It was only one time, I felt terrible,
and I started going to a different gym
before canceling my membership. Harvey,
I know I messed up big time, but my
desire was always to save us."

"That's why you changed gyms then
canceled?" Harvey shook his head in
disbelief. "If you wanted to save us then

you probably should not have screwed another guy. I've always told you to talk to me, but you never quite knew how to do that. It is such a simple thing, yet you continually shut down and look where it got us!" Harvey's anger and frustration began getting the better of him.

"Harvey I am so sorry." Andrea began to cry after burying her eyes into the palm of her hands.

"I'm sorry that this is what we've become." Harvey said in a quieted and seemingly emotionless voice.

"But baby we do not have to..." Andrea began saying.

"Okay please do not tell me what we do and do not have to do." Harvey spoke with a tone of voice angrier than Andrea had ever heard.

"So now what Harvey?" Andrea asked.

"I need time!" Harvey responded. His voice was short.

"Time for what?" Andrea questioned.

"Time to heal, to forgive! Time to see if I will be able to love you the right way again." Harvey said as he repositioned his body. Hs voice softened.

"Okay, so do you want to talk to Raina? I am sure she would love to talk to you." Andrea said.

"Of course, please put her on the phone." Harvey responded with a sort of joy that warmed Andrea's heart immensely.

"Hiiiii daddy!" Raina said excitedly as she bounced up and down on her mother's lap.

Harvey smiled. Raina certainly had a way of making his heart melt like the well churned strawberry ice cream she loved. For Harvey, loving a child was the greatest demonstration of love. "Hi sweetie, how are you?"

"I am so happy to be talking to you, and I am doing wonderful." Raina responded.

"Ha! Where did you learn such a big word?" Harvey asked as he smiled and crossed his right leg over the left.

"I heard it on television daddy! You're silly." Raina laughed and continued to bounce on her mother's lap.

"Why am I silly?" Harvey asked as he disguised his voice to be deeper than his usual speaking voice.

"Because you did not know where I learned the word. We watch television together all the time daddy. You shoulda known." Raina, for the young age of three, revealed her disappointments rather eloquently.

"You know what beautiful?" Harvey asked in a more serious tone.

"What daddy?" Raina responded.

He did not want to be the one to break Raina's heart. "Daddy is silly. You're right." Harvey took his voice up a notch in tone.

"Well, I am happier now that we are talking." Harvey smiled like a kid at Christmas opening the gift they had been expecting.

"When will I be seeing you again daddy?" Raina asked.

"What about today or tomorrow?" Harvey responded quickly.

"How about today dad?" Raina smiled.

"Of course. We have to ask mommy though."

"Yay! I'm going to see daddy." Raina yelled with excitement then slid off Andrea's lap. Raina totally missed the latter of Harvey's statement.

"Why are you yelling Raina?" Andrea asked.

"Because I am going to see daddy today." Raina smiled and hopped in authentic three-year-old form.

"Let me see the phone baby." Andrea said firmly and she placed her index finger, otherwise termed by others as her 'thinking' finger, on her left temple.

"Okay mommy." Raina quickly obliged.

"Hello!" Andrea began. Her tone spoke of 'need-to-know' curiosity.

"Hello Andrea." Harvey was aloof and his tone demonstrated his disinterest in hearing Andrea's voice.

"Are you taking Raina today? Why didn't you ask me?" Andrea unleashed a second question before Harvey could answer the first.

"If its' okay with you, I'd love to. Sorry for not asking." Harvey responded.

"It's okay! Yes, you can Harvey. What time would you like to come get her?" Andrea said while disguising hurt about their demise.

"How's 2:20?" Harvey asked.

"That's fine, I know she will love spending time with you." Andrea said in a mildly excited, yet somewhat frustrated tone.

"Thank you. I'll talk to you later." Harvey responded apathetically.

"Okay bye Harvey." Andrea said solemnly as she placed her left hand behind her head.

"His name is daddy and I want to talk mommy. Please mommy!"

"You can talk sweetie! Wait a minute, Harvey. Raina wants to say bye."

"Oh of course." Harvey responded with more excitement than in his previous response to Andrea.

"Dad let's go to the movies, to the park and then eat some French fries!" Raina said excitedly.

"Ha! Ha, we will do whatever your little heart desires." Harvey smiled as he spoke just one of his spoiling phrases.

"Okay daddy, I cannot wait to see you." Raina half-spun then sat down right where she stood-the floor.

"And I cannot wait to see you sweetie." Harvey responded with a smile that could light any and every room.

The phone call took place at approximately 9:25 AM, but 2:20 PM came quick. Raina was all ready to go. She looked beautiful, as though she was meeting the king for the first time.

Harvey pulled up to the house he once called home. He was visibly exhausted yet noticeably excited to see Raina who was in her room playing while waiting for Harvey to arrive.

"Hello there Harvey." Andrea smiled and showed those eyes she knew Harvey adored.

"Andrea!" He nodded.

"It's so nice to see you, Harvey." Andrea wore a sleek fitting dress. It was bright red, and her smile was just as bright.

"It's nice to see you also." Harvey replied, trying to keep his eyes from

71

focusing on the glamor and beauty Andrea clearly personified.

"Harvey?" Andrea called in a voice which told Harvey she had something of importance to say.

"Yes Andrea?" Harvey anticipatorily answered as he scratched his head.

"My bed is still open." Andrea usually did not struggle to be direct.

"You look absolutely beautiful, and it's no surprise or secret that I still love you deeply, but not now Andrea. Seriously not now!" Harvey's hands were now reaching towards his pockets.

"But..." Andrea continued as she moved a little closer.

"But what Andrea? Did you forget that I'm still stewing in your infidelity?" Harvey took a noticeable step away from Andrea.

"I need your forgiveness!" Andrea clenched her hands and lowered her eyes.

"And I needed your integrity. Andrea, I needed your honor. We've had countless conversations about Proverbs 31!" Harvey rebutted Andrea with intention of quieting her and ending the awkward moment.

"And Harvey, I need you." Andrea began to tear a touch.

"Really?" Harvey pulled his hands out of his pockets. The tone of his voice demonstrated, without question or hesitation, that he was frustrated.

"Yes Harvey!" Andrea remained adamant.

"I wish you needed me more before you cheated on me." Harvey made sure Andrea clearly remembered the reason their relationship ended.

"Baby?" Andrea called out again.

"Oh my-gosh! I am all ears, Andrea." Harvey had heard just about all that he could in one conversation.

"Do not forget all that we were, all that we can be, all that we had and all that we can have." Andrea looked Harvey directly in his eyes when she made this statement. Her eyes told an epic of hurt, frustration, sadness, agony, and anguish.

Harvey looked at Andrea, then back to the floor. He looked back up at Andrea, "You did!" Harvey's eyes spoke of disappointment, ambiguity, and lingering skepticism, "What else has she lied about?" He thought.

"Baby please! Listen I..." Andrea relentlessly continued. Her anguish increased as evidenced by the shape of her mouth. She knew her window of time was shrinking, and she wanted to say all she could before Harvey left with Raina. She did not know when she would have the opportunity again. But then it happened...

"Daddy! Daddy!" Raina yelled as she ran towards Harvey and gave him the biggest hug in the history of hugs, well...possibly.

"Hey beautiful." Harvey smiled, and for but a moment the world felt safe, his heart...elated. For just a moment a sense of normalcy returned.

Andrea stepped aside and absorbed the beautiful moment between Harvey and Raina. Andrea lowered her eyes. "I really messed up." I really hope Harvey finds it in his heart to forgive me and move forward." Andrea thought as she smiled at what was happening in front of her.

Harvey looked at Raina, "Hey we are outta here, time to have some fun!"

"Yeahhhhhh!" Raina jumped for joy.

"We'll see you in about 4 hours." Harvey said, giving minimal attention to Andrea as his back was almost completely facing her.

"Okay guys have fun." Andrea crossed her arms and watched them walk away. She partially smiled. She wanted Her, Raina, and Harvey to be a family-not merely relatively acquainted.

"Bye mommy!" Raina said while riding on Harvey's back. As the car drove away, something in Andrea changed. It was as if her hopes, and dreams rode along with the car which disappeared in the distance.

Raina really enjoyed the movie. They ate lots of popcorn. Raina also enjoyed a small pack of gummy worms and a strawberry icee. They had so much fun when spending time together. Harvey couldn't imagine not being a part of Raina's life. Though he did wonder how he would ever tell her that he was not her biological father. For Harvey, living a lie was not an option. However, in this case the truth would not set him free.

"I love you daddy." Raina said in her sweet voice as they were on the way to the park.

"I love you too Raina." Harvey responded with an unsteadiness defining his voice.

"Daddy, are you going to live in the house with mommy and me?"

"Not right now Raina." Harvey gave a brief response attempting to dissuade the brewing conversation.

"Why not?" Raina asked. She moved around in her booster seat and stared directly into the rearview mirror.

"Because right now mommy and daddy need to spend more time away from each other." Harvey responded. His left elbow sat on the door panel where the window automatically descended and rose, and his left hand lightly touched his temple.

"But why?" Raina asked.

"Because daddy is sad and sometimes mad, so he needs to be away." Harvey's half-frown told Raina he did not like to be away.

"Are you mad at me daddy?" Raina asked as she tucked her bottom lip.

"Definitely not beautiful. You only make me smile." Harvey responded with a full smile that warmed Raina's heart.

Raina smiled back, "Well daddy I hope you come back." She said with a hint of sadness in her voice.

"I..." Harvey's eyes lowered for a moment, but he quickly raised them to pay attention to traffic.

"Are we there yet?"

"Almost! We'll be at the park in no time." Harvey responded with excitement that almost matched Raina's.

"You're so silly daddy. No time would mean we are there now." Raina smiled and responded with authenticity for her young age.

"I am sorry, ha! We will be there in about three minutes." Harvey spoke using more definitive language.

"Okay daddy I will count."

"Okay I am listening..." Harvey raised the tone of his voice half an octave.

"One, two, three! Okay daddy we should be there." Raina counted in the cutest of measures.

"Well Raina that was only three seconds. I said three minutes, and there are 60 seconds in a minute." Harvey responded in a matter-of-fact tone as he looked back and smiled.

"Okay daddy I will just wait then." Raina responded.

"You know Raina you should try, then I will help you when you need it." Harvey encouraged.

"Okay one, two, three, four, five, six, and seven and eight, nine, ten, and..." Raina got stuck. She stared out of the window and frowned a little.

"...And eleven we are here!" Harvey yelled enthusiastically as he pulled into the parking lot.

Raina smiled. She loved Harvey's silly mannerisms.

Raina and Harvey ran around like two little kids. Harvey was a kid at heart. Harvey pushed Raina on the swing. Later he helped her move about the monkey bars.

"Let's play a little basketball dad."
Raina liked basketball, partially because Harvey really enjoyed it.

"Let me look in the trunk to see if I have two basketballs, one for me and one for you!"

"Okay daddy, but we only need one." Raina said as Harvey ran behind her towards the car.

Harvey opened the trunk, "Oh now look at that, we are about to play some basketball."

"Yay!" Raina jumped for joy. She didn't mind that her, and Harvey would have to share one ball.

"Okay Raina you take the ball first." Harvey said as he extended the basketball toward Raina.

"All right daddy." Raina said as she reached for the basketball.

"Oops I tricked ya!" Harvey laughed as he quickly pulled the basketball away.

"Daaaaaadddddd!" Raina chuckled as she ran after Harvey.

Harvey's lateral movements confused Raina. "Ha! Ha, Daddy you're too fast. I'm little!" Raina sat down near the foul line of the basketball court.

"Baby girl, are you sad?" Harvey asked.

Raina pouted as she sat on the ground with her arms folded.

Harvey knelt and touched Raina's chin; he began pulling her head upward so their eyes would be level. "Raina you cannot get..."

"I tricked you, ha!" Raina said as she quickly knocked the ball out of Harvey's hands. She ran for the ball, and so did Harvey but Raina was successful.

"You run so so so fast Raina." Harvey said as he pretended to be out of breath.

"What are you going to teach me dad?" Raina said as she stood directly in front of Harvey looking up at him – A picture worth a thousand cards.

"Well hold the ball in both hands then begin to push the basketball downward with your right hand." Harvey said as he demonstrated, with hand and body motion, what he was trying to express with words.

"Okay daddy." Raina said as she attempted to do what Harvey had asked of her.

She tried and tried and ultimately failed. She began getting frustrated and Harvey knew that he needed to intervene.

"Hey I want to tell you what the greatest basketball player said, professional or for fun like you and I ." Harvey began as he bent his knees to level his eyes and height with Raina.

Raina stared at the ground, dejected.

"Pick your head up beautiful. This is what he said: I've missed more than 9000 shots in my career. I've lost almost 300 games. 26 times, I've been trusted to take the game winning shot and missed. I've failed repeatedly in my life. And that is why I succeed."

"What does that mean daddy?" Raina asked with that adorable three-year-old blank stare.

"My dear, it simply means that you gotta keep trying, even when you're upset because you did not do something the way you wanted to you must keep trying." Harvey responded and patted Raina on the back.

"Did you ever give up daddy?" Raina asked the ear-piercing question.

Harvey contemplated on the best way to answer, "Well Raina listen to me closely, sometimes if what you are doing continues to not work then you have to do things a different way."

"Hmm okay daddy let's play some basketball."

Harvey and Raina enjoyed basketball. He taught Raina some of what he knew, but mostly the two just enjoyed the quality time spent together. They finished their outing and returned to the house Harvey once called home.

"Thanks for taking her!" Andrea met Harvey at the door. "Harvey please do not give up on Rain and I." Andrea used Raina's nickname, though rarely spoken.

"Anytime, I love her, and I love spending time with her. I will give in depth thought to you and I." Harvey responded after taking a deep breath.

"Well give me a call when you'd like to see her again."

"Andrea I've been thinking..." Harvey said as his upper teeth gripped the inside of his lip on the right side.

"About?" Andrea responded with intense curiosity. She did that one thing Harvey loved-flipped her hair then rolled the left side behind her left ear. Three seconds later she flipped the right side.

"About us!" Harvey responded as he smiled.

"Well, what about us?" Andrea tried hiding the extent of her curiosity.

"Andrea, I love you and I love what we were. I love my connection with Raina, and I just need time to heal. I trust that we will be together again, but I never want to disrespect your heart so allow me to heal and then we can try again." Harvey said as he lowered his head.

"Harvey, you have no idea how happy that makes me." Andrea said as she wrapped her arms around Harvey. He returned the embrace.

Their touch still felt magical, and the love felt as if there had never been betrayal. Harvey knew he had to face the music of the song Andrea began composing.

He sat at his piano later that night and the depth of Andrea's betrayal took him deeper than expected. He played a sad melody and cried a true cry of despair, brokenness, hurt, sadness, and pain. He finished playing but continued crying. He asked himself one poignant question, "Can I ever truly love again?"

CHAPTER 8

Harvey called Larry to schedule a time to meet up. They agreed to meet at the local diner for a meal. They hung out approximately once every few months or so. Their lives kept them equally as busy. Time organically moved but seemed to freeze for Harvey and Larry. They met at college when playing for the basketball team.

Larry worked as a tutor for the library which is where their friendship began to blossom. Harvey learned early in their friendship that Larry was a good teacher, a good listener and gave meaningful advice.

Harvey and Larry arrived at The Journey Café around the same time. Larry walked in, noticed Harvey seated close to the window near the door and walked over.

"Bro, how have you been?" Larry asked. He was usually high energy, kind and appreciative of comradery.

"I've been pretty good."

"Well, you haven't called me in at least three months." Larry was a bonafide ball-buster.

"Yeah, about that."

"I'm sure Andrea is keeping you pretty busy, but we supposed to be boys." Larry and Harvey shared the knack for dry humor. Larry embodied a quick wit which Harvey lacked.

"Talking about Andrea would open a door you'd quickly want to close." Harvey said with dark emotion.

"You look miserable bro ham, what's up?" Larry had previously been told he was a soft place to land.

"Can we talk about something else?" Harvey asked.

"That is fine with me. I am only a couple of months away from receiving my Masters of Psychology degree, just saying."

"Man, what are you just saying? Harvey laughed.

Larry laughed as well, "well..."

"Hold up Larry."

"Okay." The confusion was noticeable through Larry's tone of voice and slight squinting of the eyes and the 30 degrees turn of his head to the right.

"What does *just saying* even mean?" Harvey asked.

"Means I am educating you about some important ish, dropping jewels...you know what I mean?"

Harvey nodded his head and laughed, "No or should I say nah?" They laughed.

"Anyways, I have been learning a lot in graduate school."

"I should have gotten my master's degree for music performance." Harvey lamented his decision to only get a bachelor's degree.

"You aren't even 30 yet."

"We'll see. Business is good and the lessons are paying the bills. I think I am good for now." Harvey was typically calculated in his decision-making.

"That's great Harvey, doing what you love and getting paid to do it. Can't beat that."

"It makes work feel like I'm just having fun all day."

"Yeah, until you get a snotnose, jerky little..."

"Hey, hey now..." They laughed.

"My bad! Anyway, how many students do you have?" Larry asked.

"10 students, but the referrals continue to roll in." Harvey smiled.

"I wish I was pursuing my passion man."

"You're not even 30 yet." Harvey mocked Larry's statement from moments earlier.

"Okay, okay I deserve that one."
Larry chuckled.

"Just don't ever give up man."

"Thanks, Harv. So, what's up with you though?"

"For one I've been thinking a lot about Andrea, but I have a new student to tell you about. Perhaps I'll be telling you about her mother more than her."
Harvey's eyes brightened and widened.

"That's what I'm talking about. Let's make this boring conversation interesting. Larry readjusted in his seat. "Let's order some breakfast though, I'm famished."

"There are millions of starving children here in the United States and in many 3rd world countries. You're not famished."

Larry looked bewildered, "It was just a figure of speech Harvey."

"Yeah man I'm sorry, Andrea and Raina have been on my mind lately."

"Say more." Larry encouraged.

"I just miss them." Harvey replied.

"Are you sure that's it?"

"Honestly I can feel the pain like it was yesterday."

"I understand. Have you thought about going to counseling?" Larry typically gave logical suggestions.

"My parents did not believe in counseling, and I don't either."

"Hey, didn't mental illness run in your family?" Larry asked.

"Yeah, but why is that relevant to our conversation?"

"I just think counseling can help. That is all I am trying to say."

"I do not need counseling to deal with a break-up."

"Yet you're still perseverating on the experience."

"Come on with those big words." Harvey smiled small.

"What I am saying is that the pain from the experience doesn't seem to be going away on its own after several months, so it could be helpful to just talk it through with a professional." Larry attempted to make his suggestion less intrusive or upsetting.

"Not going to happen Larry." Harvey responded matter of fact.

"Okay just think about it sometime."

There was an awkward silence. Harvey was angry because he simply needed a listening ear and not a counseling session. "You're my friend, not my counselor or life coach." Harvey thought.

After several years of friendship with Harvey, Larry knew when to give him space.

"I'm sorry bro, I am taking my anger out on you. What do they call that in the counseling world?"

"The term is..." Larry began before being interrupted.

"Sorry, wait a minute! What do the counseling guru's call it when I take my anger out on you though I am not angry with you?"

"I believe they call it transference."

"Yeah, that's it."

"What else is going on your life Harvey?"

"Let's order our food first. I have some news for you man." Harvey changed the tone of his voice and shook his head from side to side.

"Okay, don't back out on me." Larry pointed at Harvey.

"Just wait for it!" Harvey chuckled.

They took time to look at the menu. Larry ordered blueberry pancakes with sausage. He added whipped cream on top and pineapple on the side. Harvey ordered fried fish with grits and 3 eggs over-medium. They talked between bites of food and occasionally reveled how good their food tasted.

"I think I met my next lady." Harvey shared his news.

"Wait a minute, you were just talking about Andrea." Larry challenged Harvey.

"I will always love Andrea, but she is my past. I must move on with my life."

"I won't judge or offer advice."

Harvey looked from side to side, then turned his head to look behind himself.

"What are doing?" Larry asked.

"Where is my friend and what have you done with him?"

"Oh, you real funny."

"Are you sure you're not sick?" Harvey asked.

"Okay, okay continue please." Larry laughed as he delivered his statement.

"Do you have any questions?"

"Well how did you meet her? How long have you known her? What is she like? Does she have any children? You know the usual."

"She is stunningly beautiful..."

"He could have just used stunning or beautiful, but I get it. My boy is smitten." Larry thought to himself.

"She saw my ad about piano lessons and scheduled her daughter Ariana. I only recently met her."

"That may be why feelings of Andrea are resurfacing."

"Yeah, yeah, yeah I see the alien has returned my friend to me." Harvey laughed.

"Ha, ha, you knew I couldn't resist for too long."

"Anyways, she seems funny and really sweet. She has another child, Johnathon. Our conversation flows naturally. She helped with the cookout. Larry you should have seen her at the lesson, she looked amazing."

"Oh yeah, by the way, sorry I wasn't able to make it."

"No worries, I understand."

"I hope to meet this awesome lady sometime." Larry said.

"If all goes well then there is a good chance you will."

"Hey just be careful."

"I will, thanks man. You can be annoying because you always give advice. I know you're just looking out for me."

"We are homeboys, so I care about you man."

"Thanks man, you're a good friend."

"You're welcome, you are too." Larry echoed Harvey's sentiment.

"What are you doing for the rest of today?" Harvey asked.

"I'm not sure. I may hit the gym later."

"I gotta get back in the gym. I feel like all I do is play piano."

"Holistic health, just saying, holistic health."

"I know, I will get there." Harvey patronized Larry.

"All right bro, I have to take off." Larry began ending their time together.

"I am right behind you...Just saying." They laughed.

"I can take care of the bill. You can pay next time."

"Sounds good to me, thanks." Harvey gratefully accepted.

Larry paid the bill. They shook hands, gave a bro hug with their forearms against the other's chest and the opposite arm around the other person's back. They walked out of the café.

"Let's get together again soon." Larry said as he turned back.

"Yeah, most definitely."

"Bro, I am serious." Larry laughed.

Harvey back peddled and nodded his head.

Stephanie felt rejuvenated after the cookout. The emotions she experienced, though normal, were frightening. It was the first time since Jeffery's death that she'd felt anything for anyone. After Jeffery was gone Stephanie feared falling in love again. For distinct reasons, she pondered a similar question to Harvey's, "Will I ever truly love again?"

Jeffery was her everything. He was the definition of a knight in shining armor, though Stephanie tried rationalizing her possible romantic interest: "I love Jeffery, but it's been two, almost three years since his death and I have the right to be happy. I would want him to find happiness if it were me that died." Stephanie would often reason within herself.

Stephanie was shocked, but she wondered if Harvey was a guy that she would allow herself to get to know. "Well, if he asks me out on a date, I'd probably say no." Her doubts rose to the surface.

Then she would question herself as to why the answer would be no. The answer to her question was not sensible enough to suffice. She was afraid-Afraid of loving again, losing again and the pain being too much to bear. Her father always summarized fear in this simple way: False Evidence Appearing Real. He would say, "Fear leads you to your greatest mistake, every time." Then he would tip his hat by the brim.

As Stephanie came to understand her father's statement, the greatest mistake was not believing in the potential for a preferred outcome. She mulled this decision over in her head for several hours and days and finally she derived at this conclusion, "I will give Mr. Harvey a chance if he asks." Stephanie finally conquered the fear which gripped her reality since Jeffery left.

Stephanie was ready for love. She missed Jeffery of course but could no longer hold her heart captive for a man that would never return. The long-awaited cleansing was harder than imagined. "I'm sorry Jeffery, but goodbye!" She cried, a much needed 'one last cry'...perhaps.

Stephanie never said goodbye to Jeffery because she didn't know how to let him go. Truth is, she was never ready to let him go. She cried for hours because she knew for the first time since falling in love with Jeffery, she was taking her heart back from the one who loved it best.

The night which followed would be one of the hardest yet one of the most exonerating nights of her life. "Freedom, I suppose as Frederick Douglass said, has always been costly." She reasoned as she wiped the tears from her eyes.

Stephanie went to sleep as did Harvey and for the first time they realized something wonderful-Their hearts were always sleeping under the same stars.

Stephanie slept better than she had in years. Harvey reminisced about the pain of betrayal, though something in the cosmos had changed. There was freedom, presumed agreement, acceptance that the past was just that and the future was a mystery and the most powerful choice to live for. They understood that the sphere of influence lied within themselves first and foremost.

Harvey's dad always told him, "Son if you want something in life you have to go get it." Harvey wrestled with this advice because at the core, he was passive-aggressive at best. He still loved Andrea, though a new beginning was starting to appear appealing.

He lacked confidence and assertiveness but waiting for life to land in his lap would get him nowhere.

When Harvey awoke, something felt different. He went about his morning routine and in the midst, decided to make the first step. "I'd rather step and accept where my foot lands than to not move at all." He grabbed his cell phone and dialed Stephanie's number.

CHAPTER 9

"Hello Mr. Harvey!" Stephanie laughed.

"Hey what's funny?" Harvey said sarcastically.

"Calling you Mr. Harvey sounds funny." Stephanie smiled a smile of invitation to be emotionally closer.

"You know you can just call me Harvey, right?" He missed Stephanie's subtle flirting.

"So why are you calling?" Stephanie asked as she sat up in bed.

"Well, I wanted to know if you'd like to go to dinner and a movie with me." Harvey said with a shakiness and timidity that took hold of his voice.

"Is that a question?" Sarcasm filled the air.

"I am sorry, ha! Will you go to dinner and a movie with me tomorrow night?" Harvey instantly improved on his ability to ask a direct question.

"Let me find a babysitter for the kids and I will get back to you." Stephanie said as she tried to hide her excitement.

Stephanie made Harvey wait for almost four hours before letting him know if she would be available. "Hey Harvey, sorry I am just calling back." Stephanie began apologetically.

"It's okay, I hope its good news."

"It is. My parents are going to watch the kids." Stephanie said excitedly.

"That is great news. Can I pick you up around 5 for dinner?"

"Why don't we make it 4:00 so that we have time to walk after dinner and before the movie?" Stephanie responded.

"4:00 it is. I am excited to see you tomorrow." Harvey spoke with more surety and joy in his voice.

"I am excited to see you as well Harvey." Stephanie responded.

"Wait what's your address?" Harvey said quickly as to make sure Stephanie did not hang up before he obtained necessary information.

"Oh yea. I will text it to you." Stephanie responded with slight ambivalence.

"Okay well make sure you do. I will look forward to your text." Harvey spoke with a hint of fear.

The day went by very quickly, seemingly because both had something wonderful to look forward to. Stephanie couldn't believe it. It would be the first time going on a date since Jeffery died three years ago, and for Harvey-he hadn't given another woman a second thought since breaking up with Andrea two years ago. Both Harvey and Stephanie had been hurt, though starkly different, hurt felt all the same-painful. Harvey trusted he hadn't lost his chivalrous mannerisms. Stephanie still believed in her wit and outgoing personality. She texted Harvey her address.

Night fell and both rested well. They awoke ready for the evening that awaited them. Harvey was awestruck by Stephanie's beauty, and Stephanie was amazed by the gentleman Harvey appeared to be.

Harvey did some last-minute planning for the date which he was unquestionably excited. Stephanie put on her best face and most stunning outfit. The time had come, and Harvey waited at Stephanie's front door. Then there she was, literally in all her glory. "Hi there Mr. Harvey." Stephanie said as she now stood in front of him at the front door.

Harvey was rapt as he beheld Stephanie's beauty.

"Hello Stephanie. So, shall we go?" Harvey smiled bashfully as he attempted to hide his inner thoughts.

"I am all ready." Stephanie said as she closed the door. They began walking towards the car.

"Can I get your door?" Harvey asked with a rather inviting smile.

"Well, it's not like I am going to say no!" Stephanie laughed as she lightly tapped Harvey's arm.

"Then here's to reminding you that chivalry is indeed alive." Harvey said as he opened Stephanie's door. He clenched his fist and inconspicuously pumped the air as a sign of a step in the right direction-a point scored if you will.

Harvey shut Stephanie's door then got in the car himself. He looked over at Stephanie, "Can I tell you something?" He asked with a serious look on his face.

"I believe you are going to anyway so go for it." Stephanie tilted her head slightly to the left and responded with her usual façade of sarcasm.

"Is that a yes?" Harvey replied.

"Yes, handsome it is."

Harvey smiled, "Well I was just going to say you are really beautiful, and I am really happy to be on this date with you." Harvey took in a deep breath shortly before letting out a large release of air. Being like-minded was a source of joy and comfort for Harvey.

"That was sweet of you. I am happy to be here too." Stephanie smiled, showing her agreement with the wonder of the moment.

"Seriously you wear that dress like a super model." Harvey finally mustered the courage to speak candidly about Stephanie's body and beauty.

"Well thank you. I can tell that you and the gym are somewhat acquainted!" Stephanie offered her decrepit attempt at a compliment.

"Ouch, only somewhat?" Harvey responded, revealing his disappointment.

"Hey that's all you're getting from me right now man." Stephanie smirked, knowing she had, with good intention, bruised Harvey's male ego.

"Ha! Ha, okay." Laughter appeared to be the best medicine for the sort of sickness Harvey felt inside.

They looked at each other and smiled.

"Well, I guess we better get going so we have enough time before the movie." Harvey said.

"Sounds like a plan." Stephanie responded.

They arrived at the restaurant and Harvey held the door for Stephanie.

"Hello there! Table for two?" The hostess asked with an overwhelmingly inviting smile.

"Yes please." Harvey replied.

"Okay, right this way." The hostess said. "Your server, Ruby will be right with you." She continued.

Harvey pulled out Stephanie's chair when seated by the hostess.

Shortly after being seated their waitress came to greet them. "Good evening, I'm Ruby and I will be your waitress. Can I start you guys off with anything to drink?" She asked.

"You first Stephanie!" Harvey extended the offer as a genuine gentleman should.

"Thank you. Okay well I will have a diet coke." Stephanie informed Ruby.

"Okay and for you sir." Their waitress, Ruby.

"I will have ice water with extra lemon." Harvey asked for his usual beverage of choice.

"Okay well I will be right back." Ruby stated.

"You're a true gentleman Harvey and I really appreciate it." Stephanie told Harvey without her typical and preferred sarcastic verbiage.

"It makes me happy that you appreciate me. You seem nice and sweet, and I am really...like really happy to have this chance to get to know you." Harvey responded as he touched Stephanie's left hand and allowed their eyes to meet.

The conversation paused for a moment as if Stephanie wasn't exactly sure of how she preferred responding.

"Here are your drinks. A diet coke for you ma'am, and for you sir, an ice water with extra lemon." Ruby put their drinks down. "Do you guys need a few more minutes?" She asked.

"I believe we do." Stephanie said as she looked at Harvey for approval. She took a sip of her diet coke then continued the conversation with Harvey.

"Likewise, sir. I am happy for the chance to get to know you as well" Stephanie smiled, "So shall we check the menu?" She continued.

"Yes, see I knew you were way smarter than I would ever be. Checking the menu sounds like a good idea." Harvey laughed.

"What a dry sense of humor!" Stephanie thought as she browsed the menu.

"Oh, come on, you had to think that was funny!" Harvey stated as his face dropped from the realization that Stephanie likely did not think he was funny.

Stephanie smiled, "You do have a way with humor Harvey..." She attempted to patronize Harvey's sensitive ego.

Stephanie paused, "But..." She began again...

"But what?" Harvey asked with worry.

"...But I like it." Stephanie had officially placed Harvey's ego back on the pedestal where it once restlessly rested.

"Well, that makes me feel a little better seeing as you didn't laugh at all." Harvey relayed the obvious.

"We'll get there Mr. Harvey." Stephanie smiled and lightly tapped his right hand from the other side of the table.

"You sure do have the prettiest smile that I have ever seen." Harvey offered his next compliment with a smile to accompany the words he spoke.

"Thank you very much. I really appreciate all your compliments." Stephanie replied with the level of sincerity that increased comfort between both Harvey and her.

"Stephanie, I will always do my best to build you up." Harvey replied.

"Well, that will always be appreciated." The moment was rich with accolades.

Stephanie looked back at the menu, "Are you ready to order kind sir?" She asked. Sarcasm was never too far from her lips.

"Pretty lady I am." Harvey replied. He stared at Stephanie with rather endearing eyes.

"You're pretty comfortable Harvey." Stephanie responded, revealing how surprised she was with Harvey's ability to be as open as he was with her at such an early stage in the relationship.

"You seem to have a calming effect." Harvey smiled as he found a preferred excuse for his forwardness.

"That has certainly been a work in progress." Stephanie responded and returned the smile.

"Hello lovely folks. I am sorry to interrupt, but are you ready to order?" The waitress asked.

"I believe we are." Harvey replied.

"I am ready." Stephanie replied.

"You first Stephanie." Harvey offered.

"Thank you." Stephanie smiled. "Isn't he such a gentleman?" Stephanie asked Ruby.

Ruby laughed a bit, "Yes, he definitely is. What will you be having ma'am?" The waitress continued.

"Please call me Stephanie."

"I'm so sorry. What will you be having Stephanie?" Ruby corrected her language to accommodate Stephanie's preferences.

"It's okay Ruby. I will have your Haddock with white rice and steamed vegetables." Stephanie replied as she unknowingly licked her lips.

Ruby jotted down Stephanie's order, "Oh I love this meal myself. Great choice Stephanie." Ruby gave Stephanie the thumbs up symbol. "And for you..." Ruby did not want to make the same mistake again.

"Harvey..."

"Thank you, Harvey. What will you be having?" Ruby asked while wearing a smile that was fifty percent flirtatious and fifty percent persuasion for after the meal.

"I will have your Alfredo pasta with the breadsticks and broccoli." Harvey responded. He was totally oblivious to Ruby's mannerisms.

"I think you will love that. Any appetizers while you wait?" Ruby asked Harvey and Stephanie.

Harvey and Stephanie looked at each other and the consensus was no.

"No, we will not be having an appetizer." Harvey informed Ruby. He offered a friendly smile of approval of the services thus far.

"Okay well I will put your orders in right away." Ruby assured.

"Thank you." Stephanie replied. She ran her fingers through her hair then caught a quick glimpse of Harvey. She smiled.

"Yes, thank you very much Ruby." Harvey added, missing the glance from Stephanie.

"I have to make a quick phone call. I will be right back." Stephanie moved towards the edge of her seat.

"Okay, are you? Never mind..."

"I will be right back." Stephanie smirked. She knew that Harvey would be having all sorts of irrational yet logical thoughts.

Stephanie walked away and made her phone call in the ladies' bathroom. The phone call took approximately three minutes. Harvey awaited her return and secretly hoped she would ease his curiosity about her 'emergency' phone call.

"Welcome back!" Harvey said with a smile.

"Um about that!" Stephanie began as she lowered her head.

"What?" Harvey responded, his eyes enlarged, and his teeth anticipatorily gripped the inside of his mouth.

"I actually have to go, but can I take a rain check on dinner?" Stephanie asked in a dismal tone of voice.

"Is everything okay?" Harvey asked. His eyes sank almost to his soul as he awaited what he hoped would be the answer he preferred to hear.

"Well kind of, but I do have to go and take care of a few things. I am so sorry." Stephanie said as she began walking away.

"Uh o..." Harvey began to speak as Stephanie with purse on shoulder and cell phone in hand walked away.

Harvey sat bewildered. He sipped his water, then 'stole' a sip of Stephanie's diet coke. It appeared that Stephanie did not hear him. From across the restaurant Ruby watched as the scene unfolded. The cooks were busy preparing the meal that Harvey and Stephanie ordered. Ruby wondered what was going on between the two of them. However, she had no time to investigate. She stepped into the kitchen to check on the approximate time that Stephanie and Harvey's meal would be finished.

"I see how it is..." Harvey turned around stunned. "I step away for half of a minute and you're already stealing my drink?" Stephanie laughed.

"I thought you were leaving!"

"Best first date joke ever." Stephanie began clapping while retaking her seat.

Her smile was akin to that of success. She successfully deceived a gullible man.

"That wasn't so funny actually." Harvey responded in a serious tone.

"Wait! Are you mad?" Stephanie asked, surprised.

The silence was deafening.

Harvey allowed some silence before answering, "No I'm not mad!" He wasn't smiling.

"Well, where did your smile go?" Stephanie asked, and the look on her face was that of concern.

"I'm sorry, beautiful. Here it goes." Harvey forced a smile. Inside he burned with an inexplicable rage.

"That's a little better. So where is our food? Aren't you hungry?" Stephanie asked as she totally misunderstood Harvey's body language.

"I am a little hungry." Harvey's smile was minimally more normal at this moment.

"It will probably be here soon though." Stephanie said as she smiled at Harvey.

"Do you have any brothers or sisters?" Harvey asked after sipping his water, then reciprocating the smile.

"I have an older sister and one older brother." Stephanie responded.

"Are you the youngest?" Harvey asked.

"Yes, I am. How did you guess?"

"Just a lucky guess I suppose!" Harvey winked! "Okay so who is the oldest?" Harvey continued.

"My brother Charles is the oldest, then it's my sister Dawn, then..." Stephanie began. There wasn't much emotion as she talked about her siblings.

"...Yes, the lovely Stephanie." Harvey finished Stephanie's sentence.

"I like you already." Stephanie leaned forward in her seat.

"Well, I like you too Stephanie. If all I have to do is finish your sentences, you will fall head over heels in a New York minute." Harvey smiled and leaned forward, matching Stephanie's position.

"I guess you have some work to do huh?" Stephanie laughed at her pretentious question. "So, what about you Harvey? Do you have any siblings?" Stephanie continued.

"Unfortunately, no. I'm an only child." Harvey responded as his lips almost touched and small wrinkles formed on either side.

"Hey man that's more gifts for Christmas!" Stephanie, the presumed jokester, struck again.

"Yeah, only if I cared about gifts."

"Was it hard growing up as an only child?" Stephanie asked.

"I don't know if I'd say hard, but I definitely wish I had siblings."

"How many would you have wanted?" Stephanie inquired.

"Well maybe a couple of brothers and a couple of sisters. I'd want to be the oldest though." Harvey added.

"Hmm interesting statement. Why though? Why would you want to be the oldest?" Stephanie asked while crossing her left leg over the right.

"Because I am used to leading, even if the only person I was leading was me." Harvey made another attempt at humor.

"Ha! Ha, that was funny Harvey."

"So which sibling are you closest to?" Harvey paused, "And it is about time that you laughed at one of my jokes!" He chuckled.

"All right guys here is your food." Ruby placed the plates in front of the respective parties.

"Thank you." Harvey said.

"Thank you." Stephanie echoed Harvey.

"You're welcome, guys. Enjoy!" Ruby walked away.

"To answer your question Harvey, I am close to my brother Charles. Dawn and I are a little closer in age and we seriously fought like enemies growing up."

Stephanie shook her head and looked down for a moment. "But we are better now!" She added as her body language changed-She seemed a little happier and more inviting.

"That's understandable. I think it's sometimes a lot easier to get along with the opposite sex, and the age difference set you and Charles up for a different kind of relationship than you and Dawn." Harvey psychologized the family dynamics.

"Geez Harvey why are you already trying to get into my panties?" Stephanie said with a look of frustration.

"Huh? What are you talking about?" Harvey asked bewildered.

"You're already talking about sex!" Stephanie said as she began gradually negating the frown she made.

"Okay, okay you got me...again!" The two of them laughed at the humor that was between them, even at this early stage. "How many years are between you and your siblings?" Harvey asked.

There are seven years between Charles and I, Dawn and I are two and a half years apart." Stephanie replied.

"Okay, so hey your food looks good." Harvey said.

"But yours look better." Stephanie responded. "Nice way to change the subject!"

"Beautiful lady, we can talk about anything you'd like to talk about." Harvey spoke confidently as he slid his hand towards Stephanie's.

"Watch your hand Harv, let's talk about your food." Stephanie smiled.

"Ha, well let's hope it tastes better than it looks." Harvey chuckled.

"Let's see if he shares any of his food." Stephanie thought.

"How did you become interested in playing piano?" Stephanie asked as she turned her body more to her left and she wanted to be off center from Harvey.

"When I was younger my parents played a wide variety of music, and much of my family is musically talented."

"That's pretty awesome." Stephanie smiled.

"What do you consider your talent to be?" Harvey asked, searching for similar interests and talents.

"Well, I am a pretty good dancer and I actually crochet pretty well." Stephanie replied.

"That must be pretty relaxing." Harvey decided to forego the joke about the kind of dancing that Stephanie was talking about. "It's way too early for that kind of conversation!" Harvey reasoned within himself.

"It is! I love it."

"Is it hard to find time for it with the kids and all?".

"Sometimes it is. Do you have any kids?" Stephanie replied. She scooched her butt from side to side as she readjusted for comfort's sake. She was happy to hear that Harvey was taking genuine interest in her life and her kids. "This is different!" She thought.

"Not really!" Harvey gave the dismissive, *'I'd rather not talk about that'* response.

"Not really?" Stephanie replied. She had a way of making people comfortable sharing their innermost feelings and thoughts. She had often heard, *"You are a soft place to land."*

"Well, it's a long story!" Harvey remained dismissive but opened the door for Stephanie to prod further.

"We have time." Stephanie smiled. Her eyes pierced his, and struck the nerve that makes guys say, 'I will do whatever you want.'

"Basically, my ex-girlfriend lied, told me a child was mine, I parented Raina Ari for 3 years or so then she opened pandora's box."

"That must have been so hard. Hey that sounds a little like Ariana's name!"

"I still see her occasionally. Things changed when Raina's mother found a new boyfriend. I never thought about that, but you're right-the names do sound a little similar." Harvey said as he nodded his head and squinted a bit.

"I am sorry Harvey. I could not imagine a day without my precious Ariana and Johnathan. When is the last time you saw Raina?" Stephanie asked concerned. Her mulatto face had begun turning a bright yellow.

"It's been over a year now." Harvey said as he lowered his head, clearly still bruised from the betrayal, and saddened by the absence of Raina as part of his life.

"Cheaters disgust me!" Stephanie frowned and ran her right hand quickly through her hair.

"It's nice to know that you aren't one." Harvey said sarcastically. "Tell me a bit more about your love life." He was undoubtedly smitten by Stephanie's beauty and mannerisms when she spoke.

"Really?" Stephanie never liked talking about past relationships.

"Why not?" Harvey shrugged his shoulders.

"So, what do you want to know?" Stephanie braced herself.

"How long have you been single?" Harvey started with a basic and somewhat easy question.

"3 years or so." Stephanie responded.

"What happened?" Harvey asked.

"Long story Harvey, long story!" Stephanie stared blankly out of the window beside their table.

"Like you told me, we have time." Harvey laughed.

Stephanie did not return the laughter. The silence was defeating and needed to be broken.

"Um different question-Have you ever been married?" Harvey asked.

"Okay I am just going to tell you. This is hard to say, but I was married to Jeffery for 7 years before he died in a skiing accident. Prior to the accident he miraculously beat cancer. I was 20 when we met. We were married by 22, and I was pregnant with Ariana by 24, almost 25. He died when I was pregnant with Johnathan. Now I am a 29-year-old widow. And now here we are. Sometimes you should watch what you ask because the answer may not be what you are prepared to hear!" Stephanie's attitude worsened, understandably so as her broken heart was not yet mended.

"Wow I am so sorry for making you relive all that." Harvey responded, "It breaks my heart that you had to go through that." Harvey felt deflated.

"It's okay, I guess talking about the past is necessary sometimes." Stephanie eased Harvey's conscience.

"I guess you're right." Harvey smiled as he felt a little better about the conversation they were having.

"Anyways, I never asked, but how old are you, Harvey?" Stephanie gracefully changed the subject.

"I am 31. I've already passed the big 3 0." Harvey said as he looked away making evident, his embarrassment.

"I am right behind you man so do not even start talking like you're old." Stephanie laughed and tapped Harvey's shoulder from across the table.

"For what it's worth you do not look a day over 25." Harvey smiled while delivering the timely compliment. With both elbows on the table, Harvey held his chin with his right hand and looked Stephanie in the eyes.

"I will take that as a compliment." Stephanie smiled, but quickly moved her eyes.

Harvey leaned in closer, "You definitely should take it as a compliment..." Harvey spoke with increasing confidence which continued to grow as the date went on.

"And why is that?" Stephanie asked with a grin that solidified her joy for this sort of engagement.

"Because it is a compliment. I was absolutely hitting on you just now."

"Maybe I'm embarrassed to say this, but I kind of liked it Mr. Harvey. Or should I say old man Harvey." Stephanie chuckled profusely.

"Hey watch it," Harvey smirked. Sounds like we are off to a great start Miss Stephanie." Harvey leaned back on his seat.

"What other questions do you have up there in that head of yours?"

"Let's see, how's your food?" Harvey asked, "I figured I would give you an easy question this time!" Harvey's wide smile returned.

"Very good, thank you. How is yours?" Stephanie replied.

"I was just about to ask the same question!" Ruby interrupted, accompanied by a more genuine smile than before.

"My pasta was especially good." Harvey responded.

"Can I get you guys more to drink?" Ruby asked.

"Yes please." Stephanie said.

"I will take more water with lemon. Thank you, Ruby." Harvey added.

"I will be back in just a moment. No rush, but do you want me to bring the check? Ruby asked.

"Yes, that will be fine." Harvey responded.

"I will be right back."

"Okay!" Harvey responded.

"Who taught you to be such a gentleman?"

"I'd have to say my parents."

"That's neat. Are they still married?" Stephanie smiled and tilted her head slightly to the left.

"They are. What about your parents?"

"My dad moved out when I was 17." Stephanie's eyes met with the plate in front of her.

"That's too bad! I am very sorry to hear that. I can see that his leaving still bothers you."

"Thank you, it was hard, but I'd say it made me stronger." Stephanie's eyes never stopped staring at the plate during this conversation.

"Here you go guys. Here are your drinks and the check. I'm sorry I forgot to ask; did you want any dessert?" Ruby said hurriedly as she had to make her rounds to other tables.

"I don't!" Harvey said as he looked at Stephanie.

"I'm all set! You've been great, thank you."

Ruby smiled, "All right I will be back for the check whenever you're ready." Ruby said as she walked away.

"Would you like to for a walk soon?" Harvey asked with confidence that Stephanie would answer yes.

"That sounds nice!" Stephanie replied.

Stephanie and Harvey finished their drinks. Harvey paid for his and Stephanie's meal then they went to walk. The walk was nice and somewhat romantic. It was time for the movie and Harvey was especially excited because he loved basketball. Stephanie had agreed to watch *The Crossover that Won the Game*- The movie based on actual events, written by Jamell Ponder and his brother.

"I heard that this movie is supposed to be really good." Harvey said.

"I heard that as well." Stephanie replied. "Do you play basketball Harvey?"

"I do! Do you play?" Harvey hoped for a yes so that he could offer a challenge.

"I'll show you my skills sometime if you're up for it."

"Ha, we'll see!" Stephanie passively accepted the challenge. "Are you ready to go on in?" Stephanie asked.

"Most definitely." Harvey responded as he touched Stephanie's hand lightly. She looked at Harvey and smiled but did not accept the covert handholding suggestion.

Harvey and Stephanie walked into the movie theater and prepared to watch the long awaited, *The Crossover that Won the Game.*

CHAPTER 10

Harvey and Stephanie sat quietly through the movie. Except for Harvey's random comments because he had a small problem of talking through movies. "Did you see that move?" He would say. "Shhh..." Stephanie would politely respond.

The silence would return for a moment, but Harvey simply could not help himself. "All that dad does is work. He needs to spend more time with his family." He would look at Stephanie to see if she was paying him any attention, and more times than not she would be focused on the movie.

"Harvey I am trying to watch the movie!" Stephanie would say wearing the brightest frown-smile possible.

They enjoyed the story and especially how the movie addressed bullying and the importance of forgiveness. Harvey certainly appreciated the way the relationship improved with the main character and his father. Stephanie related well to the hardworking mother that often felt she was doing everything by herself. For Stephanie it was more than just an absent father. In her case it was the father who would never return despite the deepest desire to never leave. Her heart broke for the boy in the movie particularly because the movie was based on actual events. Harvey loved basketball so seeing the development of the main character's skillset interested him. The emotional maturity also stood out to both Harvey and Stephanie. And of course, a coach that takes a vested interest in the well-being of a child is always a great thing.

"Okay you have to admit, that was a good movie." Harvey proclaimed as they walked out of the theater.

"I do agree sir." Stephanie replied. "Your excitement is adorable!"

"Thank you. What was your favorite part?" Harvey asked as they walked towards the car.

"Hmm let me think..." Stephanie paused. "...Okay I think my favorite part was when he saved the life of his coach who was really his..." Stephanie began.

"Hey, hey, hey do not give it away for other people that may read the book or watch the movie, but yeah that was a really awesome, unexpected addition to the story."

"What was your favorite part of the movie?" Stephanie asked.

"I kind of liked when he gained his confidence and made the winning shot." Harvey responded.

"The story really did show an amazing sense of emotional development." Stephanie responded rather matter of fact manner.

Harvey and Stephanie made their way to a nearby park bench. Stephanie called and informed her mother she would be a little later than expected. Her mother loved her grandchildren and never cared how long they stayed at her house.

"You've got to admit it, the crossover and dunk in his last high school game was ridiculously phenomenal." Harvey said. He turned to Stephanie in excited when he delivered this statement.

"Oh my, did you really just say ridiculously awesome?" Stephanie asked.

"I definitely did, and I am not taking it back. Actually, what I said was ridiculously phenomenal." Harvey corrected Stephanie with a slightly obnoxious tone and smirk.

"Great choice of words Harvey. That's all I can say about that." Stephanie added girl flavor to the humor of the moment.

"Ha, well then I'd say you've said enough." The two of them laughed after Harvey attempted to add the finishing touches to the conversation.

"What did you think about the twist with the mom and coach?" Stephanie asked.

"I think it was kind of creative. It certainly wasn't really expected. I liked it though."

"I liked it because of how important Coach Crossover already was to Shay." Stephanie added with a nod of approval for that element of the story.

"It was definitely a well-done story." Harvey added.

"Maybe we will have to play a game of basketball sometime." Stephanie extended the challenge.

Her smile could make any man's heart melt, but when it came to competitiveness Harvey was no stranger and accepted all challenges, "Girl, I will take you to school." Harvey informed Stephanie.

"Then I will be your student."

"Seriously I enjoyed this time with you and hope to see you again sometime outside of piano lessons."

"I think we can make that happen. I'd like that Harvey. You were a total gentleman this evening and you're a cutie too." She ran her fingers through either side of her hair.

"Hmm cute guy with gorgeous girl? Sounds about right..." Harvey paused. "We should most definitely make future dates happen!"

Stephanie and Harvey walked towards the car.

"Can I get your door beautiful?" Harvey asked with his hand already reaching.

"Yes, you may, handsome." Stephanie replied.

Harvey drove Stephanie home and they said their goodbyes which concluded with, "I will see you at our lesson in a few days."

"See you soon Harvey." Stephanie said.

Then the two of them hugged goodbye. "Bye!" Stephanie said as Harvey got closer to his car.

"Bye!" Harvey smiled and waved after turning around.

"It was nice to actually be treated like a lady for once in a long time." Stephanie smiled.

Stephanie picked up the children. Like any involved mother, Stephanie's mother asked about the date. Stephanie and her mother had a great and open relationship.

Stephanie took the kids home and got them ready for bed.

"Hmm that was surprisingly pleasant. I totally thought he was going to be some shy nerdy dude. He was sweet and nice to spend time with. I am interested seeing him again." Stephanie said aloud as she walked towards the bathroom.

Harvey cruised along listening to whatever songs were on the radio at the time. "She is a very nice girl and I'm looking forward to getting to know her better. And she is so beautiful as well. This could be the start of something wonderful. I guess I will just see where it goes." Harvey told himself. He smiled and tapped his hands on the steering wheel totally on rhythm with the music on the radio.

The rest of the night went by smoothly. Harvey stepped outside and stared at the night sky. Love appeared to be in the air.

Stephanie looked up into the night sky to thank God for sending Harvey into her life. The moon and stars wept. One could not be completely sure of what the tears represented, but nonetheless they wept.

That night, once again Harvey and Stephanie slept under the same stars. Was love in the air? Would the moon and stars agree with their ensuing romance? What did the constellations know that Stephanie and Harvey had yet to discover? Perhaps only time could reveal. Where love laid, hate was present also awaiting a slight shift in the emotional experience.

CHAPTER 11

"Well, hello there Ariana!" Harvey said with a smile.

"Well, hello there Mr. Harvey." Ariana spoke with her mother's brand of sarcasm-mimicking, echoing, repeating what's been said to them.

"And hello to you Stephanie." Harvey smiled as his eyes glanced quickly at Stephanie.

"Hello there Harvey." Stephanie returned the smile as she raised her purse further on to her shoulder.

Harvey and Stephanie shared smiles only they fully understood.

"Are you ready for your lesson today?" Harvey asked as he lightly touched Ariana's back.

"Yep, I have been practicing." Ariana skipped her steps a bit.

"Practicing your scales?" Harvey asked in a higher pitched voice toward which a child would gravitate.

"Yep!" Ariana smiled.

The piano lesson went very smoothly. Harvey considered the lesson to be a success.

"You are certainly an amazing and natural talent Ariana."

"Thank you, Mr. Harvey."

"You're welcome, Ariana." Harvey patted Ariana's back. "You've been practicing?" He continued.

"Of course. Mommy makes sure that I do." Ariana responded in a cynical voice.

"Well thank you mommy." Harvey said sarcastically as he looked at Stephanie and smiled.

"You're welcome. My little girl's growth is important." Stephanie tried disguising her excitement about seeing Harvey.

"Isn't my mommy awesome Mr. Harvey?" Ariana asked innocently.

"She definitely is."

"You guys are both too kind." Stephanie lowered her eyes in embarrassment and downplayed the praises.

"You must know how awesome you are Steph!" Harvey said boldly as he touched her arm.

"Thank you very much, but I am paying you to teach my little girl mister." Stephanie laughed. "Yeah, and not to give me compliments

"Oh yes let me get right back to that." Harvey smiled then turned back to the piano.

The room erupted in dishonest laughter.

"Ariana, will you play a C-Major 7th for me?"

"Here you go Mr. Harvey." Ariana began to play exactly what she had been taught.

"Very nice. Do you know all your chords?" Harvey asked.

"No Mr. Harvey I do not. I would like to learn though." Ariana responded.

"The best students are the students with a desire to learn." Harvey said as he smiled and nodded.

"What does 'desire' mean Mr. Harvey?" Ariana asked while looking bewildered.

"It means that they want to learn." Harvey tried to speak in a manner that a child could understand.

"Ha! Ha well alright Mr. Harvey I do know what 'want' means." Ariana smiled.

"Then you know what desire means."

"You're nice Mr. Harvey." Ariana said, then reached up to tap Harvey's shoulder.

"Thank you, Ariana, so are you." Harvey turned and looked at Stephanie,

"You heard your daughter-she says I'm nice." Harvey smirked then stared as if to await a response.

Stephanie shook her head and motioned for Harvey to continue the lesson.

"Ariana, mommy doesn't like our talk breaks."
"Nope!" Ariana laughed and rocked back on the piano bench.
"I totally love how well Harvey and Ariana interacts." Stephanie thought.
"Okay Ariana I will demonstrate your chords for you." Harvey informed Ariana.

Ariana was very attentive to all that Harvey said and did.

"I think I can learn that by next week, Mr. Harvey." Ariana told Harvey.
"If you practice the right way then I believe that you can too." Harvey had a way with encouraging words.
"Okay Mr. Harvey I will practice just the way you played it."
"Well Ariana that is a good start." Harvey tilted his head slightly to the right.

There was a brief silence.

"Hey, I will see you ladies next week." Harvey continued.

"Yes, you will." Ariana smiled a smile that Harvey would never forget.

"If I'm lucky I will see you this weekend." Harvey whispered in Stephanie's ear.

Ariana pouted, "Heyyyyyyyyyy, no whispering. Not fair!"

Stephanie pulled Ariana in close to her, "I will call you." Stephanie smirked and chuckled lightly.

The rest of the day went by rather quickly. It was time for Stephanie to put the kids to bed. After that it would be time to rest after a long day.

Before bed that night Harvey thought about what he and Stephanie could do this weekend. He texted Stephanie just before bed, "goodnight I look forward to seeing you this weekend. Give me a call tomorrow night once you are settled." Harvey hated text because genuine emotion could not be deduced.

"Goodnight! I will call you tomorrow." Stephanie sent her brief reply.

The night breezed by, and the following day did not present many challenges.

Stephanie assisted Ariana with her homework and helped Johnathan with just about everything because he was only three. Admittedly potty-training Johnathan was a little easier than when she potty-trained Ariana. Johnathan was almost ready for regular underpants and to say goodbye to diapers once and for all.

Periodically Ariana got mildly frustrated with writing her ABCs and numbers, though Stephanie certainly had the patience of a mother. "If you stay calm and keep doing your best you will get it baby." Stephanie would often say.

"Ugh it's so hard mom." Ariana would say, then cower over in a sort of fetal position.

"Well think of it like practicing piano."

"But it's not fun mommy." Ariana rebutted.

"But you do not understand everything immediately when learning something new on the piano, correct?" Stephanie attempted to strengthen the correlation for Ariana.

"I do not mommy." Ariana's fetal like positions would persist.

"Sweet girl, you just keep trying and trying and trying some more until you understand it, correct? And please sit up straight. You are not a baby!"

"Sorry mommy!" Ariana sat upright in the living room chair. "Yes, you are right mommy."

"So, do you know what I am trying to tell you?" Stephanie asked.

"To keep trying?" Ariana responded.

"What a smart little girl. You're exactly right." Stephanie high fived Ariana, gave her a hug then kissed her cheek, "I love you." Stephanie added.

"I love you too mommy..." Ariana paused, "This much!" She stretched her hands as far apart as she could.

They sat and ate dinner together. Conversation between family members was pleasant. After two years Stephanie had gotten pretty good at desensitizing herself to the empty chair beside Ariana. She missed Jeffery yet tried removing him from the core of her heart. The unadulterated truth remained; his heart was made for hers and hers for his.

Even at the age of three Johnathan looked so much like his father. Ariana had many mannerisms that reminded Stephanie of Jeffery-The way she chewed her food, her laugh, the way she told jokes, the way she rose back to her feet after falling - she even crossed her little arms and pouted somewhat like Jeffery. Johnathan hadn't shown many mannerisms yet, but he was still young, and Stephanie figured Johnathan would eventually exhibit mannerisms like Jeffery.

She tucked Johnathan in his soccer bed, then proceeded to tuck Ariana in. Like every other night, she read the book of Ariana's choice.

On this particular night it was "Only you can control your future; Sometimes you will never know that value of a moment until it has become a memory; Sometimes the questions are complicated, and the answers are simple; You'll miss the best things if you keep your eyes shut; and unless someone like you cares an awful lot, nothing is going to get better. It's not."

Stephanie read a quote that preceded Ariana's heart-warming words. Stephanie repeated the quote that meant most to her, "You will never understand the beauty of a moment until it has become a memory."

Ariana yawned, then rubbed her eyes one after the other. She then delivered her final words before going to the place Stephanie called dream world, "I love you so much mommy, but I miss daddy." Ariana said as she proceeded to close her eyes.

"I love you too." Stephanie kissed Ariana's forehead. Just that fast Ariana had fallen asleep. "I miss him too dear; I miss him too." She wiped tears which began falling. She did not want to cry anymore, but she understood it as a normal part of grieving.

Stephanie looked over to make sure Johnathan was sleeping safely and soundly, then she walked out of the bedroom. It was not going to be a good night and she knew it thanks to Ariana's raw emotion and propensity toward transparency.

"How can I move on when my husband holds my heart? How can I bring another man into Ariana's life after she became so close with her dad? Can anyone love her the way her dad did? There is simply no replacement!"

Stephanie's thoughts moved a mile a minute. Harvey was a worthy contender, though Stephanie and Jeffery did share a once and lifetime kind of love. She knew she had to open her heart, but she wasn't sure how to. It was almost as if she believed Jeffery would be back some day. She liked Harvey, she really did, but wasn't sure continuing to pursue getting to know him was best at this time. "How do I tell this wonderful man, who I've started something with that we have to stop because I'm still in love with a dead guy?"

Stephanie knew that she sounded ridiculous. She doubted many people could relate or understand her unending, unrivaled love for Jeffery.

"There are some people you are meant to love forever, and I think Jeffery is the person I was meant to love forever. But why did you have to die?" Stephanie hit the headboard with her left hand. "We were supposed to raise our kids together!" She began to cry, "Jeffery why did you have to go? We were supposed to grow old together! We had so many dreams and goals. When Ariana goes to her senior prom where will you be? When she starts dating Ariana will, no I, no wait...we will need you. When she gets married who will give her away? I hate you Jeffery, but I love you just the same. The thin line per se. Anyways, I don't even know what I am saying. Why did you have to go?" Stephanie hit the headboard again then threw herself on her bed and dropped tears into her pillow.

It felt as if Jeffery was listening and responded, "I am sorry. I wish I had not gone skiing that day."

Stephanie wiped her tears, but they flowed victoriously, "Nothing can bring you back. Not a sorry, not a wish, not a prayer, not a do-over, not an I love you though baby, I so deeply love and adore you."

The wind blew and the leaves rustled the tree. Stephanie remained silent adhering to the longing of her heart, "If you only understood how much I love you." She felt Jeffery's presence.

"Well, you know what? I cannot fully love a dead man. Life does not offer do-overs. You're gone and..." Stephanie began weeping more powerfully. "...And you are never coming back!" Stephanie buried her face in the pillow.

In that moment Stephanie heard Jeffery say, "I love you my sweet Stephanie. No matter how far away I am, I will always be right here. I'll never leave you baby." For just a moment the pain lifted, only to instantly return.

"You have no idea how much I miss you and the children. I wish I could be there to grow with all you!" The ghost of Jeffery spoke.

"Jeffery, baby stop it. Please Jeffery let my heart go. I must let go of you, but I honestly have no idea where to begin. You were lovely and awesome, and we were awesome

The presence in the room eased slightly, then placidly returned, "Forever darling, forever. I'm sorry." Then the manifestation, and illusion of reunion ceased.

"Goodnight and goodbye Jeffery." Stephanie looked at the empty side of her bed, clenched her pillow tight then closed her eyes. They shared a love so strong that even death was no match.

The moon and stars stood still. Would Jeffery ever release her heart? Would Stephanie ever have inner peace?

CHAPTER 12

Stephanie awoke exhausted from the emotional night she had. Today was a new day and she would make the best out of it. She did not know exactly what that meant for her. She'd lost sight of what truly made her.

She was making a valiant effort to let go of Jeffery, but to no avail. Then there was Harvey. Stephanie figured he deserved a chance, but also understood love wasn't based on charity. She felt that she had to end what they'd only just began. She was certain of nothing, yet hopeful for much. Stephanie could tell Harvey was a rather amazing man, but her heart wasn't ready for what he was offering. The pertinent question was: would her heart ever be ready? Stephanie cried so many nights and she missed Jeffery more than words could express. He was gone, but not forgotten. He could never be forgotten. Their once in a lifetime love defied all rules of time and space. He was missed, yet most amazing; dead, yet very much alive; buried, yet ever present.

He lived on in her subconscious and reigned within her conscious. Jeffery was no longer living, breathing, speaking, yet still made her laugh, cry, smile and frown. He made her feel good when she was down and brought her down when she was feeling good. Jeffery possessed grave-like love-Even from the beneath the ground his presence was felt, and the continued effect was evident.

There he lay, slowly decaying in a pine box covered with dirt and flowers decorated the tombstone commemorating his honor and memory. Jeffery Pullman rested in her heart, walked in her shoes, cried her tears, and felt her fears. With every smile she felt him. With every breath she remembered their love, their fights, and the man she had come to adore. She recalled all that they shared. She longed to have it back. With every cry she loathed him yet loved him all the same, "Why aren't you here Jeffery? I need you so much." Then she'd cry some more at the memory of the man she still loved. "I hate you!" She would sometimes say. She blamed him for their unhappy ending. He would never escape the blame for all that would go wrong, could go wrong and what had already gone wrong.

Jeffery once held her hand, kissed her forehead and said, "I pray that you always *dance as if no one can see you, love beyond words, and sing as if no one can hear you.*"

Stephanie never forgot those words. Amid her remembering, Harvey maintained his own agenda. The good morning texts and random conversation throughout the day lead to the question he had been waiting to ask since Ariana's piano lesson, "Are you free this weekend? If so, will you accompany me to the park avenue festival?"

Stephanie answered with the best intentions possible, "Yes I'd love to." She smiled and Harvey did the same. "That's great! How is Saturday at one o'clock?" Harvey asked.
"That time works for me handsome." Stephanie responded. She scratched her scalp and wore a face wrought in confusion.
"See you Saturday beautiful."

The next few days went by quickly for Harvey, though for Stephanie those days felt like weeks. They texted quite often throughout the week and spoke on the phone twice. The conversation was normal.

Saturday had finally come. Harvey was excited to take Stephanie on another date. He showered and put on the outfit he had picked out two days earlier. He styled his hair the same as he did for their first date. Stephanie previously commented on how much she liked the hairstyle Harvey wore on their first date.

He wore tan Ralph Lauren Khaki pants and shoes from the same designer. The shoes were brown with white and tan designs. His shirt-a long sleeve white button up had tan and white cufflinks, with patterns on either pocket. The back was designed with calligraphy style writing. Harvey arrived at Stephanie's house at approximately 12:55 PM. He knocked on the door but received no answer. He called, but again, no answer. His text went unanswered, and his second call went to voicemail also. Eventually Harvey went to the festival by himself. He wasn't sure why Stephanie stood him up but avoided overthinking – this time.

It was one o'clock and Stephanie sat in front of Jeffery's tombstone with flowers sharing her best words, "Jeffery I needed to come to see you at least once more. I am supposed to be on a date right now. In fact, he is probably at the house wondering where I am, if I am alright and if I am standing him up or not. I feel sorry about all that, but I needed to be near you once again..." Stephanie paused. The winds blew lightly after thunderstorms threated to fall, then the sun briefly appeared. Stephanie released her greatest cry since Jeffery's death and their untimely demise.

The weekend inflexibly moved along. Now it was Tuesday, and time for Ariana's lesson. Still no word from Stephanie, but Harvey thought for sure he'd see her on Tuesday, and she would have a simple yet logical explanation for her. Much to his dismay and surprise Stephanie no called-no showed for Ariana's lesson.

Patience had expired, and it was time for answers. Now Wednesday had come, and Harvey felt compelled to act. He called and was surprised when Stephanie answered the phone, "Hello Harvey." Her voice sounded groggy as if she had been sleeping or crying, or both.
"Well, well, well, hello. What's been going on lately? What happened Saturday?"
"It's really hard to explain!" Stephanie said in a lethargic voice.
"Well, I hope you'll try, I have all the time in the world." Harvey was undoubtedly frustrated.
"I just cannot see you anymore."

"What? Can you tell me why?" Harvey asked frantically. "I thought that things were off to a good start between us.

"Things did get off to a really good start, but at this time it is better if we go our separate ways for now." Stephanie quickly choked back tears to disguise her hurt. Her right hand and palm gripped her forehead while the left hand rested on the living room window.

"I think I deserve more of an answer than what you're giving me."

"We all think we deserve something. Truth is we are deserving of nothing." Stephanie said while thinking of her happily ever after which turned into goodbyes, tears, funeral arrangements, and the vanishing of the body she loved to touch.

"I know we didn't have a chance to spend much time together, but I really like you and I'm not ready for this to end." Harvey pleaded for a second chance.

"I am ready for this to end, and Harvey I am deeply sorry, goodbye." Stephanie did what she thought best.

"Stephanie! Hello...Hello..." Harvey's voice was met by the blank air. "I cannot believe this. I was the perfect gentleman and now this?". The phone call ended, but Harvey wasn't sure when Stephanie hung up on him.

Harvey was appalled at what just happened. He attempted the classic call back a few times before accepting what he wanted is not what she wanted. He did the safest and healthiest thing he could; he left her alone. She lingered in his thoughts, and likewise he remained in hers.

He mulled things over in his head for a few days but knew that he would have to make at least one final call.

CHAPTER 13

Harvey made his final plea for a chance at Stephanie's heart. The phone rang several times, but to no avail. A voicemail was his only option, so he held nothing back when leaving the heart piercing voicemail. "Every once in a great while you meet someone you just know you're meant to share something with. I know we just began, but I do not want it to end. I know you're special and I genuinely want to get to know all that makes you who you are. I understand that a new relationship could be challenging, uncomfortable and even a bit scary, but I'm willing to go the extra mile if you'd give us a chance. Regardless of your decision please do me one favor, *dance as if no one can see you, love beyond words, and sing as if no one can hear you.*" Harvey concluded by leaving the rather unexpected ending to his voice message.

Stephanie had been so preoccupied with work, the kids, and her toxic thoughts that it took her 3 days to listen to voice messages. She heard Harvey's message and was not moved until he said, *"dance as if no one can see you, love beyond words, and sing as if no one can hear you."* It was then that she crumbled to tears. It was at this moment and this moment only Stephanie realized she was missing one man due to the memory of another. She was missing a chance for new love due to the retention of a love that could never return. Her past had become her present, and her present had become her past. The future was a mystery, but the past wrote its own version of the story. She feared moving ahead because of the pain and guilt of truly leaving Jeffery behind. It appeared that even from the grave Jeffery wanted to be her future. Unfortunately, without living he could only be one of these elements to her; He could be her past, no matter how wretched or beautiful, a memory is what Jeffery would be reduced to. Could she carry him without losing herself?

Once the busyness momentarily subsided Stephanie sat disconcerted, pondering the events which transpired in less than one week. She had a decision to make, and it had to be soon. She grabbed her phone and began the process of calling Harvey. She put her phone down as she did not know where to begin. She had no idea if Harvey would allow her back into his life or simply reject her. Stephanie feared beginning something new, the in-between, the beginning and the end.

Harvey awaited Stephanie's call, but eventually relinquished hope. He was sad, but he honestly understood.

Harvey was no stranger to love. Regrettably, he was no stranger to loss either. He understood both quite well. Likewise, he understood hurt and disappointment. He wanted love, but after Andrea shattered his heart, hopes and dreams, he wasn't sure he could handle another heartbreak or heart ache. Another heartbreak could catapult Harvey to his breaking point, consequently incinerating the nobility he held dear.

Andrea altered his beliefs about relationships, though he was no longer afraid to love, trust, hope or dream again. He wanted to build life, share life, and create life with someone special. He wanted to be life to her, and her to him.

He wanted to mean the world to someone, be the reason someone smiled, and to wipe tears away when necessary. Self-actualization wasn't enough, he desired love. He longed to be her safe-haven, consider himself the lucky one, to write 'our notebook' while on the longest ride of their lives; always offering the best of themselves to one another.

Harvey figured love may not be in the cards for him. He sure hoped so, nonetheless according to his warped philosophical paradigms he didn't believe he would find love.

Since love was out of the question, Harvey depended on his music as a source of comfort. He played songs such as *Ain't No Sunshine by Bill Withers, End of the Road by Boyz to Men, Back at One by Brian McKnight, Cupid by Sam Cooke, A Woman's gotta Have It by Bobby Womack, Don't Wanna Miss a Thing by Aerosmith, Cruisin' by Smokey Robinson, and several classical songs, At Last by Etta James, Kiss from a Rose by Seal, Say Something by Christina Aguilera and A Great Big World. Harvey ended with a couple of modern 'top forty' songs.*

Like anyone expressing genuine emotions, they ebbed and flowed along an all too familiar range.

He began giving minimal thought to writing a romance novel like a man he admired, Nicholas Sparks, the 'love guru'. "He'd periodically say, "One day Sparks...One day!" But that dream would quickly fade as the reality of his true talents came to mind.

Harvey played his final song of the night then laid down for bed. He tossed and turned all throughout the night. Then at 4:37 AM his phone rang,

"Hello..." Harvey sounded as if a hand was partially covering his mouth.

"Harvey, I am so sorry to call at this time of morning. It's just that I can't stop thinking about you." The caller began.

"Okay I am seriously half asleep. Is this Stephanie?"

"Yes, it is. Can we meet to talk sometime?" Stephanie asked with a certain level of sincerity that moved Harvey.

"Sure! Text me or call tomorrow evening." He did not want to show excitement, but the sound of Stephanie's voice radiated a smile.

"Okay I will. Thank you and again I am sorry for the pain I've caused."

"You're welcome, no need to apologize."

"There is reason to apologize, but we can talk about that another day. Goodnight Harvey."

"Goodnight Stephanie."

8:00 PM came and Stephanie was all settled for the night. She wanted to call Harvey and watch a few of her favorite television shows. Stephanie went to her contacts list and scrolled until she reached Harvey's name. She stared for a few moments. She battled ambivalence and joy all at the same time.

"Hello!" Harvey answered. Stephanie couldn't see his smile on the other end of the phone.

"Hi Harvey, how are you?" She twirled her hair to fend off nervousness.

"I am pretty good." Harvey responded in monotone.

"That is good to hear."

"I was kind of glad that you reached back out to me." Harvey began.

"Only kind of?" Stephanie asked. Her sense of humor had not faded.

"Well yeah because you left so suddenly before."

"I am sorry Harvey."

"It's alright. I understand. Not saying I was happy though." Harvey began speaking with a slightly deeper voice.

"I have been doing a lot of thinking and I'd love to get together sometime." Stephanie replied.

"What's been on your mind Steph?"

"Just life."

"You gotta give me more than 'just life' Stephanie!" Harvey said candidly.

"My past relationship, also you and I."

"Okay." Harvey replied in brief.

"I'd like to tell you everything, but more than anything I miss you and I miss 'us', whatever that was at such an early stage."

"For what it's worth, I miss 'us' also."

"What time can you meet this Saturday?" Stephanie asked.

"How's three?" Harvey responded.

"Three is good. Is the park by 5th Avenue and Burlington a good place to meet?" Stephanie asked.

"That works for me." Harvey smiled, looked up towards the ceiling and thanked God.

"Harvey?"

"Yeah?"

"I am really looking forward to seeing you again." Stephanie spoke with newly found sweetness in her voice.

"Thank you." Harvey smiled, "I will see you Saturday."

"No um...Ah never mind." Stephanie began.

"You can say it."

"No, I will see you Saturday." Stephanie responded,

"See you Saturday." Harvey was colder than Stephanie expected.

"Bye Harvey."

"Bye Stephanie."

Saturday came fast. Three o'clock came even faster. Stephanie waited at the tree next to the Rockwind Pavilion as discussed with Harvey. He had always been a man of his word, and today was no different.

Harvey arrived close to the time of their scheduled time to meet. Stephanie's beauty was radiant than ever before. He wondered what she looked like approaching the tree by which she awaited his arrival. She stood in command of the moment. She stood as a queen awaiting her king, a princess awaiting her prince, perhaps just a girl awaiting the right guy to help heal the broken places. Harvey, on the other hand walked with uncertainty.

He dared not compliment her so soon, but she was beautiful, she was amazing, but this wasn't easy. He wanted to give up, though somehow knew she was worth it. As Bob Marley so eloquently said, "If she's amazing, she won't be easy. If she's easy, she won't be amazing. If she's worth it, you won't give up. If you give up, you're not worthy...Truth is everybody is going to hurt you; you just have to find the ones worth suffering for."

"Hello Harvey!"

"Hi there Stephanie."

"Can I just say that I've missed you?" Stephanie spoke with a level of timidity she'd not forecasted.

"You can say whatever you like!" Harvey smirked.

There was a short pause in the conversation.

"I've really missed you too Stephanie."

"I hope we can pick back up where we left off." Harvey wasn't sure what caused Stephanie to change, but he liked it.

"I hope we can make it work this time." Harvey responded.

"But why now? Why me?"

"Because you're awesome and I really like you. I see something really special in you and in us." Harvey said as he looked Stephanie eye to eye.

"Harvey, I want to try." Stephanie spoke directly. She hung her head briefly then smiled small.

"Why?" Harvey asked. He once heard a speaker say, "What is most important is not the answer you receive, but rather the questions you ask.

"Because you're the greatest, the sweetest and the best guy for me now." Stephanie responded.

"Now?" Harvey pondered. "So, what will stop you from running away this time?"

"Because I know that I'm not ready to let you go. I want to know if what I feel is real and if what we have started is worth finishing." Stephanie appeared ready to risk so much for the sake of love. She moved a little closer to Harvey on the park bench.

"I want to try as well. Thank you for giving this another chance." Harvey's smile was akin to kid in a candy store.

"Thank you very much for not giving up Harvey. I know I did not make things easy for you." Stephanie responded. She shook her head from side to side. She was disappointed in herself, yet gracious to herself because she understood the unavoidable journey on which she embarked.

"Ha! Ha, no you definitely did not."

Stephanie commenced speaking but decided silence was the best response.

"I guess it was all part of the process huh?" Harvey asked.

"Yes."

"Well, I suppose tomorrow is called 'the gift' because you never know what it may bring." Harvey passively forgave Stephanie's offenses. He put his arm around Stephanie as if to further show that amends had been fully made.

"I'm glad it brought me you, Harvey!" Her smile was sincere. She believed she could be happy with Harvey.

"Well let's continue creating awesome tomorrows." Harvey said with an inviting tone.

"I'd like that." Stephanie responded.

They hugged then stared each other in the eyes. The magic resurfaced, though tragedy trailed not so far behind. They fully intended to dance in the rain, but what would be the damage done? Collateral and otherwise? Harvey and Stephanie anticipated fighting for happiness. At what cost? This was the question no one asked. Would there be pain in the pleasure felt? Or perhaps pleasure in the pain felt? They would pursue love. What would be the calculated loss? What amount of pain is too high a price to pay, too heavy a burden to bear?

Some would say they needed each other for a pick-me-up of some sort. Falling is always the unappreciated, unwanted, and unworthy adversary.

Stephanie never fully explained her prior decisions, but Harvey chose not to focus on having all the information. Moving forward was the goal, and they would move into the abyss, perhaps into their glory days, maybe the forsaken, but certainly the mysterious. They had no clue what lied ahead of them, but discovery was the goal.

"Welcome to your new day," the heavens spoke. All earth would know of their love. All would know their names, their joy and their demise.

CHAPTER 14

Love was in the air and the time to experience it was now. "Hey beautiful lady, can I see you tomorrow?" Harvey smiled and leaned over his kitchen sink, looking over the back deck him and his dad worked so hard to build.

"Definitely handsome." Stephanie smiled on the other end of the phone. "Want to meet at 3:30 at my house?" She continued.

"That sounds good."

"Okay I will see you at 3:30." Stephanie checked her hair and makeup in her bathroom mirror. "I am not so beautiful!" She thought.

"Okay beautiful."

Stephanie smiled and was awestruck by Harvey's impeccable timing.

Harvey was excited to begin spending time with Stephanie again, but he wasn't totally at ease with their decision to resume. He knew he'd show up. Would she?

Knock! Knock! Harvey waited for the door to open. "Hey, Mr. Harvey what are you doing here?" Ariana asked. She bounced and moved in for a side hug.

"Hey there Ariana. I came to spend time with your mommy." Harvey said as he returned the hug and added a smile.

"But it's not time for our Tuesday lesson." Ariana said innocently.

"I know, but..." Harvey began the sentence that he had no idea how to finish.

"Ariana enough with the questions!" Stephanie interjected.

"It's okay Steph."

"Harvey no it's not." Stephanie said sternly.

"Mommy!" Ariana called out.

"You know I do not like whining girl."

Ariana hung her head and walked away slowly.

"How has your day been?" Stephanie asked after taking a sigh of relief.

"Can I say something?" Harvey asked.

"Um I guess!" Stephanie laughed.

"You were somewhat dismissive of Ariana. I think she just wants your attention."

"Ah I know, I know. I just get so agitated sometimes." Stephanie shook her head. "Do you think I am a bad mother?"

"No not at all. I just wanted to point out that Ariana wants and needs your attention. That's it!" Harvey smiled.

"Already telling me how to parent, geez." Stephanie laughed. "Anyways, thank you. I will keep that in mind. Now how has your day been?" Stephanie smiled and clasped her hands in front of her.

"Ha, yes beautiful it has been good. How has yours been?"

"Busy with the children." Stephanie forced a look of exhaustion on her face and slumped her body temporarily.

"Hmm I can only imagine."

"Why do you want to date someone with children?"

"No one is perfect. It's about seeing how a person's life aligns with mine." Harvey delivered the almost perfect answer. It was lacking in perfection because he said nothing about his intent to exclusively date a specific woman with children-Stephanie.

"I would have to agree..." Stephanie unclasped her hands, clapped twice, and smiled.

Harvey nodded...

"Ariana and Johnathan have a playdate with my friend, Julie this

160

afternoon so we can have some alone time." Stephanie tilted her head slight to the right and fixed a naughty smirk upon her face.

"I like that idea, but eventually you know I will have to bond with them as well." Harvey responded totally missing any innuendo whatsoever.

"I know, I don't want to rush it though." One thing Stephanie feared since Jeffery's death was bringing a new man into the lives of her children and hurting them if the relationship failed.

"I understand. Whenever you're ready." Harvey was known for his patience and understanding.

"I believe the time will come and we will know." Stephanie answered quickly.

"What do you think about walking the beach, then eating ice cream?"

"I love that idea. Just to warn you, I am a total beach bum in the summer." Stephanie cocked her head slightly left and put both hands on her hips.

They talked, shared a light meal, and randomly played with the children. Julie arrived to pick up the children with the expectation that Stephanie would get the kids after her date with Harvey. Stephanie and Harvey arrived at the beach and decided to get ice cream first.

"How's your chocolate and vanilla twist?"

"Really good, thanks for asking. How is your vanilla with caramel?" Stephanie inquired.

"The best thing ever."

"Hmm I can tell that you really love your ice cream!" Stephanie teased.

"Is it on my face or something?" Harvey said with a serious tone.

"Oh yes, let me get that for you." Stephanie said as she ran her hand across Harvey's face. "Ha! Ha, just joking." She continued.

"Silly girl, but I must admit, it was cute though." Harvey paused, "I am looking forward to our walk together. And in terms of you touching me, feel free to do so anytime." Harvey smirked and nodded. The sexual innuendo was subtle yet pronounced.

"I am too. Hey now, there may be time for touching, but not yet. Be patient hot pants, I'm a lady!" Stephanie smiled as she gently placed both hands on her hips and rolled her eyes.

"Hey, you were the one who touched me..." The two of them laughed together, gave a quick hug, a brief stare then smiled.

They finished their ice cream then began moving along the pier. They overlooked the water and embraced the setting sun.

"I'm glad to be here with you."

"It's nice to be here with you as well. I have a pretty good feeling about this." Harvey added.

"Me too Harvey, me too."

"Can I hold you in the gazebo facing the sunset?" Harvey asked. It had been a while since he had experienced romance, but Stephanie was the focus of his affection.

"Yes, handsome you can." Stephanie smiled. It had been a while since she had been held.

"I am really excited to hold you in my arms." Harvey said as he rubbed Stephanie's back.

"It's been a long time since I've been held so I know it will be nice." Stephanie put her arm around Harvey's back.

"Mmm..." Harvey lightly moaned, "I am happy that I can be your next." They paused and shared a look of approval about the next steps that were quickly approaching. One to the other, their smiles connected.

The two of them smiled at each other and continued towards the gazebo. Stephanie laid in Harvey's arms, and it was like Heaven had returned to earth.

The moment was sweet and memorable. They looked over the horizon and all was well. Love had entered their world.

"Ice cream, a nice walk, cuddling in the gazebo overlooking the horizon-I'm happy, but there's more fun to experience." Harvey interrupted the serene silence.

"How so?" Stephanie asked.

"There's a place just up the road, makes the best pies ever. Would you like to go?" Harvey asked.

"Of course, and by the way you're smiling, the pie must be 'to die for'. What is your favorite pie anyway?" Stephanie asked.

"To die for?" Harvey pondered, "Anyways, I'd have to say good ole classic apple pie."

"Warm?" Stephanie asked.

"It definitely has to be warm for me to get my full enjoyment out of it, ha!" Harvey chuckled.

"I'd have to agree. I really believe you have a love affair with apple pie." Stephanie covered her mouth to mute the small laugh that developed.

"I promise to never betray you with apple pie." Harvey laughed, though Stephanie did not. "What's your favorite kind of pie?" Harvey asked.

"Hmm let me think...I am definitely a lemon merengue pie kind of gal." Stephanie smiled and licked her lips. "Even talking about it gets me all out of sorts!" Stephanie shook her head, ashamed to have joined Harvey's obsession in some way or another.

"Good choice, good choice. Uh...who has the love affair?" Harvey cocked his head back a little which added a flare of humor to his response.

The conversation hit a lull, then Harvey delivered a somewhat expected 'guy' statement. "I bet you taste just as wonderful." His face wore a serious stare because he took a shot in the dark, not knowing how Stephanie would respond to his forward statement.

"Would you like to find out?" Stephanie asked. Something felt right about the mood. The moment lent itself to a desire just to be close to someone, anyone, and in this case that 'someone' was Harvey.

"I sure would beautiful lady." Harvey said confidently.

They stopped in their tracks. It was only slightly dark, and the cars moved about, seemingly without no regard for anyone but themselves. Harvey looked at Stephanie, and she looked at him. "I've thought about kissing you for so long."

Harvey deepened his voice and spoke lower than his normal volume.

"I won't stop you!" Stephanie said as a kid awaiting her first piece of birthday cake.

Harvey grabbed Stephanie by the arms and pulled her closer. He slid his hands to the upper part of her back, and she wrapped her arms around his waist. Then the moment was almost heightened by passionate and sensual kissing.

"I could get used to this, but let's wait on the kissing Harvey." Stephanie said through the smile she wore.

"I really hope you do. You're worth waiting for."

They arrived at the pie store and completed their orders. "How's the lemon?" Harvey asked.

"The lemon?" Stephanie asked. She looked confused as her right hand rubbed her temple.

"Yes, the lemon!" Harvey replied. He was oblivious to the reason that Stephanie was confused.

"Um, yeah, uh what about the merengue?"

"Matter-of-fact much?" Harvey smirked.

"I am!" Stephanie laughed. "Now what are you asking about?" She continued.

"Fine! How is your lemon...your lemon merengue pie? Excuse me!"

"It's great! Thanks for asking." Stephanie teased a bit.

Harvey shook his head at Stephanie's audacious behavior.

Stephanie tasted her piece of Heaven then asked, "How is your apple pie Harvey?"

"Ha, it's freaking amazeballs. Never thought you'd ask." Harvey laughed.

"Oh...my...gosh! Do not ever say amazeballs again." Stephanie barreled in laughter. "You are not in high school! You look young, but not that young!" Stephanie's laughter continued.

The two of them laughed the night away. They sat on the pier, in multiple gazebos, laid on the beach and walked sweetly hand-in-hand. The moment was perfect.

It was moments like these that they never wanted to end. Certain universal laws would always apply: The law of gravity-What goes up must come down; the law of time-What begins must end. What is born must die; the law of rhythm-everything has its tides, everything rises, and everything falls; the law of cause and effect-action precedes consequence. To become the master of your destiny you must master your thoughts, yourself. You create your reality.

Further every thought has a direction, a destination as governed by its conduit. The mind is a powerful instrument and love embodied impure supremacy. How far would one go to satisfy the yearnings and presumed privileges of their mind and emotions? The answer is found only in the element called time, the use or misuse of knowledge and response to what is felt-Pity, fear, joy, disgust, pain, love, hate, sadness, and so on. While the payment for immorality is demise, the reward for virtue is merely anecdotal.

CHAPTER 15

Stephanie arrived at Julie's house to pick up Ariana and Johnathan. Upon entering she noticed an unfamiliar man sitting in the living room.

"Hey Julie, I'm here for the kids."

Johnathan ran over to Stephanie, yelling, "Mommyyyyy." He gave Stephanie a big hug.

Ariana, on the other hand seemed preoccupied.

"Hey, how's my big boy doing?" Stephanie smiled. "Girl if you don't get your butt over here and give me a hug, I'm gonna..." Stephanie said as she focused her attention on Ariana.

Ariana laughed then hurried over to Stephanie; they embraced.

"Okay my loves, play a little longer while mommy talks to Julie."

"Soooo how was it?" Julie met Stephanie near the front door.

"The date was amazing. I think he's a good guy. I have a good feeling about him."

"Tell me more..." Julie used the typical 'gossip girl' approach

"He's sweet and yes, a gentleman. I can tell he really likes me."

"Sooooo, I cannot remember if I've asked you already, but is he cute?" Julie giggled like a middle school girl.

"Harvey is so handsome! Yeah dorky, but cute." Stephanie concluded.

"And how..." Julie proceeded but was interrupted.

"Excuse me, I do not mean to interrupt, though I couldn't help but introduce myself to the beautiful young lady standing in the kitchen. I'm Brian!"

"Nice to meet you Brian, I'm Stephanie." She turned back to Julie and thought little of Brian's random interaction.

"She's dating someone Brian!" Julie interjected.

"I heard that she went on a date. Anyway, I am just introducing myself." Brian gave Julie a look that said, "Calm yourself please."

"Anyways, it is nice to meet you, Brian. I might see you around from time to time at Julie's." Stephanie was nice, but dismissive.

"I hope so. Have a good night." Brian displayed his mesmerizing smile. Then walked back into the living room.

"Who is that guy?" Stephanie asked.

"One of my brother's friends. He's a total hottie, but he's never appealed to me as relationship material."

"Hmm well whatever. I don't even care to know why he's at your house." Stephanie replied.

"Harvey sounds like he's worth giving a chance."

"Girl, thank you so much for babysitting. We will have to get together sometime." Stephanie said as she moved in for a quick hug.

"We will girl. We will!" Julie said.

"C'mon kids let's get ready to go." Stephanie called out. She was exhausted and ready to catch up on sleep.

Stephanie stepped into the living room and got the kids ready to go.

"You sure are amazingly beautiful. I really hope to see you again." Brian attempted to woo Stephanie before the opportunity passed him by.

"Thank you, but I really have to go. I really am flattered; I just don't have time for whatever this is." Stephanie turned away and headed for the door.

"Right on Stephanie. Have a wonderful night." Brian said.

"You too Brian." Stephanie turned back only a little.

Stephanie walked out of the house, put the kids in the car and headed home. She slept wonderfully that night. That Brian guy slipped in and out of her thoughts, but Harvey stole the show. He impressed her. She had every reason to be hopeful about the future. Her justified belief was that Harvey would be there with her. Besides Jeffery, Harvey was the sweetest man she had ever met. She looked forward to further getting to know him.

CHAPTER 16

A few days passed, and though now dating, Harvey and Stephanie decided to continue Ariana's piano lessons.

Ariana played gracefully and had grown immensely since beginning lessons with Harvey. It had been several weeks of lessons, but it felt like many more. For a 5-year-old, her understanding of theory and musical application was quite good. There was great hope for her being an amazing talent someday; even more so than now.

Weeks passed. Harvey and Stephanie continued to see each other. This time they went to the drive-in movie theater and shared a large bag of popcorn.

"I really feel like movies are becoming our thing!"
"Ha, I was thinking the same thing." Stephanie laughed, then smiled while she laid on Harvey's chest.

"We should be watching the movie beautiful!" Harvey said jokingly.

"Once again I was thinking the same thing." Stephanie laughed.

"I'm glad you amuse yourself." Harvey was completely captivated by Stephanie.

"Do you like the movie?" Stephanie asked.

"It's absolutely adorable." Harvey ran his fingers through Stephanie's hair and kissed her lightly on the cheek.

Something happened in that moment. Stephanie looked at Harvey; He looked back at her. Harvey leaned in and Stephanie moved closer. Then finally it happened, the moment every new couple waits for; the first kiss. Their lips met; their hands moved. Harvey played with Stephanie's hair, and she gripped Harvey's neck. The magnitude of the moment was overwhelming. Whatever movie was 'watching them' became nothing more than background noise. Brian became merely a fleeting thought.

Now back at Stephanie's house she laid on Harvey's chest against the car.

"Hey Stephanie?"

"Yes Harvey?"

"I want more of you." Harvey said without hesitation.

"What do you mean?" Stephanie asked, only a touch confused.

"I cannot continue seeing you this way."

"Okay, I'm confused." Stephanie replied.

"What I am saying is that..." Harvey paused, and as intended, the anticipation increased.

"Come on, tell me handsome." Stephanie poked Harvey's arm.

"Stephanie will you be my girlfriend?" Harvey's question was more anticlimactic than Stephanie imagined.

"Aw Harvey, I would love to. You had me worried."

"That makes me happy. I am so happy to call myself your boyfriend." Harvey's face told the tale.

"And likewise, heyyy you're my boyfriend, my boyfriend." Stephanie sang joyously.

"Can we do dinner with your kids sometime to let them know?"

"At some point, yes. For now, we could just spend more time together with the kids. They both love going to the park."

"I like that good idea." Harvey replied.

"We could take them to the park in a couple of days." Stephanie said after running through her calendar in her head.

"I say we do it." Harvey smiled.

"It's a date handsome boyfriend." Stephanie smirked.

"I cannot wait lovely girlfriend..."

"Too much mush!" Stephanie said after a brief pause.

Harvey and Stephanie laughed much of the night away. Sometimes they had no clue what they were laughing at. The adage states laughter is like a medicine. It must be true because healing began on the night of May 21st. Hope for tomorrow was present and it hadn't been for quite some time. But now there was hope, there was joy and a haven where they could surrender their heart with one reasonable request-honor my heart!

They slept.

CHAPTER 17

"Good morning beautiful!" Harvey said through the other end of the phone.

"Good morning to you as well handsome. It's nice to hear from you so bright and early."

"What can I say? I woke up with you on my mind." He wanted Stephanie to be the first person he talked to when he woke up and the last person he spoke to before going to bed at night.

"Then I'd say you are off to a good start to your day." Stephanie said starkly.

"I hope you were thinking of me also."

"Well of course. You're my new boyfriend. How could I not think of you?" Stephanie's smile was genuine and her statement authentic.

"That's what I like to hear." Harvey responded as he puffed his chest a bit, resituating in his bed.

"Do you have a busy day ahead?" Stephanie asked.

"I have 4 students lined up so..." Harvey replied.

"So, kind of busy?" Stephanie asked almost rhetorically.

"Hmm, yeah I suppose so." Harvey replied.

"But that's good though!" Stephanie's voice was a little higher in tone.

"No worries, dear, I am not complaining." Harvey laughed.

"Ha, have to keep those bills paid."

"That's certainly an understatement, beautiful." Harvey spoke vaguely of the struggles for middle class Americans.

The conversation was flowing well but eventually slowed.

"So, what are you up to after work?" Harvey asked his leading question.

"I'm not sure yet. Why?"

"Oh, just wondering when you were going to invite me over for dinner." Harvey asked with such decorum.

"How about one day next week?"

"That sounds great." Harvey sat up in bed and smiled.

"What would you like for dinner?" Stephanie asked. It had been a while since she cooked for a man, so naturally, she was slightly nervous

"Can I think about it and get back to you?"

"Of course, you can handsome." To some extent Stephanie felt the pressure ease.

"Thank you. Do you have a busy week ahead?" Harvey asked.

"Eh somewhat. What about you?" Stephanie had become good at giving generic responses that lacked detail.

"I do, but I'd love to go for a walk with you Saturday." Harvey said.

"That sounds nice!" Stephanie smiled. "Can you be available Friday night?"

"Anything for you beautiful."

"Really? Anything?" Stephanie teased, and she immediately began thinking how to bring Harvey's statement to life-House repairs, mowing, more home projects, massages or even better, spa days, babysitting, car repairs, though she came to this resolve; authentic love was enough.

"Yes really, anything!" Harvey responded in an animated manner.

"Okay good because I may invite you over Friday night!"

"I have a confession..." Harvey was ready to test Stephanie's level of security or insecurity perhaps.

"What is it Harvey?" According to Stephanie's perspective confessions were never a precursor to good.

"Are you sure you're ready for it?"

"What is it?" Stephanie asked with frustration in her voice.

"I was just going to say that I secretly do hope you invite me over." Harvey eased Stephanie's illogical yet understandable beliefs.

"Whew! You had me worried. That's no secret and it is hardly a confession." Stephanie laughed.

Harvey joined in the laughter, "Well anyways..." Harvey paused.

"It's okay to be at a loss for words Harvey because it's time for me to get ready for work anyway. I gotta get the kids ready also."

"Okay well I am looking forward to seeing you soon." Harvey said.

"Me too handsome!"

Harvey smiled at Stephanie's kind words, "Have a great day Steph." He spoke through the smile which persisted.

"You too Harv!"

"Harv is really not all that acceptable as a nickname." Harvey laughed.

"What? Why not? And you think Steph is a cutesy nickname?" Stephanie asked as if sadness had suddenly come over her.

"Whatever, it just isn't!" Harvey responded stoically.

"Well now I am disappointed!" Stephanie pouted as her arms fell by her side in defeat.

"But you can call me anything you want to." Harvey quickly added to the diminishing conversation.

"That's better. Hey text me later, okay?" Stephanie was now running behind.

"Okay beautiful I will. Have a great day and I will talk to you later."

"Bye handsome. Have a great day."

"Thanks, bye Steph!" They laughed.

CHAPTER 18

The week went by smoothly. Brian appeared to have disappeared from Stephanie's thoughts completely. Harvey and Stephanie's excitement grew as Friday quickly approached.

There was nothing like young love-The butterflies and sweet eyes. The talking day and night, even when words escaped them. Sweet nothings, smiles, blissful anticipation of what's to come and the upward commute towards cloud nine. As the law of gravity says, "What goes up must come down" - They would eventually fall.

Friday finally arrived. Harvey and Stephanie texted throughout the day, though she had yet to invite him over. She had developed a knack for making Harvey wait. Eventually she did ask.
"Do you want to see me tonight?" Stephanie asked the long-awaited question.

"It's about time you asked. I'd love to babe. What time?"

"Any time after 7!"

"That gives me a little more than a couple of hours. That time works for me." Harvey masked his excitement by talking about details.

"So, will I see you later?" Stephanie asked.

"Definitely! Let's say around 7:30 at your place."

"That sounds great. I will be waiting for you Harvey."

"I cannot wait to see what all this anticipation brings." Harvey attempted to extract information from Stephanie.

"I guess we will just have to wait and see." Stephanie replied in a mysterious manner.

The next 2 hours or so were full of mundane tasks and mental preparation for the time they were about to spend together. The time had come, and Harvey arrived clearly dressed to impress.

"Whoa you look really good Harvey." Stephanie leaned in for a hug.

"Ha, do not sound so surprised." Harvey hugged Stephanie, then leaned in for a light kiss.

"I'm not surprised hun, you've just never gotten this dressed up for me."

"I'm just messing with you Stephanie. I understand." He marveled at their identical gullible nature.

"Let me pull up our old text thread about dinner..." Stephanie paused, "...Okay here it is. I believe you said you wanted Alfredo pasta with broccoli and chicken wings."

"I believe you are right. You're a fun texter by the way."

"What does that even mean?" Stephanie laughed at Harvey's peculiar description of her communication.

"Just all the emojis and shorthand writing and all, it's kind of funny."

"No one has ever said that to me. You must be a thinker or something." Stephanie teased once again.

"As a matter of fact, I am." Harvey said proudly.

"Should I be concerned?"

"Concerned about what?"

"Uh I don't know."

"Don't worry, I am a thinker; I think mostly about you though."

"I'm okay with that." Stephanie stared into Harvey's eyes and touched his hand. Harvey grabbed her hand and kissed it; His eyes barely leaving her gaze.

"So where are the kids?"

"They are with my mom."

"Are they close to their grandma?"

"They love, love, love their grandma and she love them." Stephanie moved her head slowly from side to side.

"What about your dad?"

"He loves the grandchildren also, but they have a uniquely special bond with grandma."

"Ah well children usually do develop a unique connection with their grandmothers. Maybe it's because women are more nurturing." Harvey responded matter-of-factly. "You'll have to tell me about your family sometime."

"I'd like to hear about yours as well."

"I am an only child, not much to tell." Harvey minimized the importance of talking about himself as it pertained to his family.

"Sure, there are. Did you ever wish you'd had brothers and sisters?" Stephanie was determined to get Harvey to open up to her.

"I used to, but not so much anymore. I vaguely remember us talking about this." Harvey tried finding a way to avert the topic.

"I think you're right, but that sounds depressing. Why don't you wish you had brothers and/or sisters?" Stephanie asked.

"I just got used to being an only child." Harvey was becoming more uncomfortable with the topic. He had never been very good at talking about himself.

"So which parent are you closest to Harvey?" Stephanie seemed to ignore Harvey's discomfort.

"I'd have to say my dad. I was always a daddy's boy." Harvey answered definitively.

"Are you close with your mother?"

"Kind of, but not so much." The disfigured look on Harvey's face showed that Stephanie finally hit a sore topic of conversation.

"If you do not mind me asking, why not?"

"Can we talk about that another time?" Harvey's tone was dark.

"Sure!" Stephanie decided it was time to let up. "I did not like your tone though Harvey. I think I upset you!"

Harvey drifted into thoughts about his childhood experiences. His mother, a Christian woman yet brutal. She would say things like, "I always wanted a girl." She was not supportive of Harvey's interests. He later learned that she treated him according to how her dad treated her. And well, the corporal punishment...Those are some of the many experiences Harvey locked away in the depths of his innermost being. He understood resurrection could lead to death. How exactly, remained a mystery.

"Harvey, hey Harvey..." Stephanie snapped Harvey out of his reverie.

Harvey shook his head, "I'm here."

"I said that I was sorry to have upset you."

"Sorry, I am not upset. It is just tough for me to talk about my mother!" Harvey paused, "So which parent are you closest to?"

"I've gotta say it's equal."

"C'mon it cannot be equal! Really?" Harvey asked.

"Yeah, I really think so. I mean mom and I have a special bond, but my father is my rock. He moved out once, but eventually returned. He spoiled me, but more so with amazing love. I feel blessed." Stephanie answered with absolutely no emotion or tonal variation in her voice.

"Awesome!"

"I hope to meet your parents sometime." Stephanie added.

"I'd like to meet yours also."

"You will at Ariana's 6th birthday party."

"Maybe I can bring my parents to the birthday party." Harvey shared his idea. Truth be told, he wasn't ready for Stephanie to meet his parents.

"You should. The more, the merrier."

"Done!"

"What is something you enjoy doing?" Stephanie asked.

"I like..." Harvey began.

"Wait!" Stephanie interrupted.

"Ha! Aye, aye captain."

"It can be anything besides play the piano."

"No!" Harvey said in a sarcastic and peculiar tone. "Well, I like to write periodically."

"Hmm I want to read some of your writing sometime." Stephanie paused, then Harvey interjected.

"I'd love that. I also like playing basketball."

"I would school you." Stephanie said as she deepened her voice and laughed.

Harvey looked from side and turned 360 degrees, then pointed at himself, "Who? Me?"

"Unless there is some paranormal stuff going on inside these walls, I am talking to...you mister! I doubt I am seeing people or hearing things."

Harvey looked away briefly then resumed looking at Stephanie. "You're hilarious. You should audition for *The Next Comic* Standing."

"What will be funny is when I take you to school and make you cry like a wittle baby!" Stephanie cocked her head to the right, flicked her long blonde hair and waved her finger from side to side.

"Okay you're really funny, not to mention...really cute."

"Cute? Who are you calling cute?" Stephanie changed to a more serious tone.

"Uh...Uh..." Harvey was at a loss for words.

"And have you seen how good I look on the inside?"

"I really want to." Harvey thought to himself.

"Aren't you going to say anything?" Stephanie continued.

"I meant that you're beautiful and...

"Harvey, Harvey stop." Stephanie chuckled softly. "I'm just teasing."

"I am going to get you." Harvey laughed as him and Stephanie began to playfully tussle.

They stared into each other's eyes, both feeling the magic of the moment. It was a moment worthy of a Polaroid picture in a frame on the wall. It was just that, a beautiful moment.

Harvey broke the silence, "So what about you? Same question-what is something you like to do?"

"Hmm I like hiking."

"Is that how you keep your figure so...?" Harvey flirtatiously licked his lips.

"Are you already checking out my body?" Stephanie asked with a devilish smile.

"Um it is in front of me." Harvey laughed while delivering his direct answer.

"Keep your eyes to yourself mister." Stephanie teased.

"Do you mean that?"

"Maybe…"

"We should go hiking sometime." Harvey quickly changed the subject.

"I would like that."

"It will be fun."

"Harvey, can I ask you something without you getting upset?"

"Sure!" Harvey said timidly and with hesitation.

"What happened with your mother that makes it so hard for you to talk about her?" Stephanie softened her voice as she asked this question.

"She…she…Listen I do not want to talk about this. I love her, but she is the cause of so much hurt and disappointment. She almost cost my parents their…their…okay whatever I am not talking about this. Maybe I will tell you more sometime!" Harvey took a deep breath, then forced a smile back onto his face.

"Okay Harvey well thanks for the little that you did share. I hope you came hungry." Stephanie lightened the mood with the promise of food and a compliment.

"Indeed, I did." Harvey responded.

"One plate coming right up Mr. Harvey." Stephanie half-smiled through her teasing. She didn't care for Harvey's guarded demeanor, but she tried to understand.

"My stomach is anxiously awaiting its due filling, sexy." Harvey returned the compliment.

"No need to wait much longer." Stephanie said as she turned around and placed Harvey's dinner on the kitchen table. She then did a cute dance, turned around, grabbed her plate, and placed it across from Harvey's plate.

"You have siblings, right?" Harvey asked.

"I am pretty sure we talked about this, but yes, I do; two to be exact. I have older brother and one older sister. Are you sure you're not an old man?" Stephanie's sarcasm never missed a moment to shine.

"Hmm okay, whatever smart mouth!" Harvey smiled, "Who are you closest to?" Harvey continued.

"Dawn and I grew closer over the years after we learned how to fight less. Charles didn't really have time for his sisters when we were growing up. He was out being 'macho' with the guys." Stephanie accentuated and emphasized 'macho'. He eventually began spending more time with Dawn and I which brought Charles and I closer.

Harvey took his first bite. "Stephanie, oh Stephanie!" Harvey shook his head.

"What?" Stephanie asked.

"This food is the bomb." Harvey eased Stephanie's concern.

"Thank you and I am sure no one says, the bomb anymore." Stephanie smiled.

"Oh, uh…You're welcome."

"What do you want to do after dinner?" Stephanie asked.

"Do you have any good movies?" Harvey truly did love movies, but he knew this would allow him to be close to Stephanie.

"I have a decent selection to choose from."

"Now here is the million-dollar question-Do you have any popcorn?"

"Don't push it buddy." Stephanie laughed.

"I'm a popcorn fan so I had to ask."

"Handsome, why don't we start by choosing a movie?" Stephanie requested.

"Ha, all right I'm fine with that."

They browsed through Stephanie's movie collection. They agreed on a few different movies. There were comedies, romance, action and a few real-life stories. They decided on a movie called *Tainted Love*. They enjoyed the writer's creativity and aptitude for embodying original thought. The weak nature of the protagonist disturbed Stephanie. She couldn't believe all she'd gone through and her tedious journey toward strength and healing.

And, well, there were times the movie watched them. Harvey and Stephanie kissed passionately. They touched like it could be their last.

Harvey was moved by the gentle nature of Laney's (i.e., the protagonist) boyfriend. He wanted the two of them to succeed in their relationship. He certainly hoped the antagonist, Jackson would get his due punishment for his crimes committed.

They were alone and close, therefore exploration of the body next to you was highly probable. Harvey kissed Stephanie's neck and she moaned his name. Their lips met, then the real magic commenced. Harvey touched Stephanie in places she'd somehow forgotten belonged to her. She touched him in places he had not been touched in several months, maybe even longer than a year. What happened next would forever remain between them.

They cuddled and Stephanie proposed a challenge. "I know you like to write from time to time. I would love for you to write a synopsis of the movie. I am curious as to how you would summarize Tainted Love."

"I can do that." Harvey immediately accepted the challenge.

"Now?" Stephanie applied pressure.

"Hey, you didn't say right now, ha." Harvey laughed and shook his head.

"Will you write it now?" Stephanie asked.

"Sure, let's see if I can entertain you with my gift, but only because I like you!" Harvey smiled.

Harvey labored deep in thought, but his thoughts failed him.

"I have faith in you hun. Just keep trying. I am going to step away and crochet while you think."

After a few more moments it came like someone had handed the synopsis directly to him. "Here it is beautiful:"

"Ooh let me see!" Stephanie said excitedly.

SYNOPSIS:

23-year-old LANEY METRIANAS has her evening shift interrupted by a friend from college, JACKSON OWASCO whom she hadn't seen in 2 years. Though happy to see Jackson, Laney was devoted to her responsibilities while at work. Jackson, a vagabond wanted to hear all about Laney's life. Laney, a sweet soul with a personality to brighten anyone's day was far too kind to deny a "harmless" friend a chance to talk about life-past and present. Regardless of Laney's feelings, Jackson, a man with a wicked soul was determined to get exactly what he wanted. What began as innocuous dialogue led to a night neither Laney nor Jackson would ever forget.

BRIAN BAKER, a 25-year-old man that put the 'R' in romance, the 'L' in love and the 'H' in hero has the level of commitment necessary to steal Laney's heart. From the moment Brian laid eyes on Laney it was love at first sight. Laney made him labor for her attention, affection and ultimately her heart. Brian was awestruck. He asked for a name, but instead received silence and Laney's back as she walked away.

Brian was no quitter. He did the unimaginable, the 'never-done-before', and his reward was well worth the effort. Unfortunately, the exterior does not reveal

195

how life may have dragged someone through mud by which they are still stained. Laney once strong-now made weak, once secure-now apprehensive, once happy-now wretched, once whole-now broken! From a young age Brian's father, JACOB BAKER taught him to protect and serve. Laney gave him the chance to show all that he was made of.

Brian loves Laney as best he knows how. He arises as the 'Knight in Shining Armor', but much to his dismay the demons Laney battled immobilized him short of victory. Feeling dejected, he became the definition of what he despised, a defeatist.

Just as Laney was recovering and rising above the cloud resting over her, Jackson obtained a job where she worked, Delicate Delights Diner. As the pieces of her world began fitting together again, the person who shattered the functional boundaries reared himself again. The strength Laney thought she had, failed when the boss, having no knowledge of her turmoil demanded Laney remain at work alone with Jackson.

As the story unfolded, heartbreaking news catapulted the relationship of Laney and Brian toward destruction. The power of love drew them back together. Love compelled and love won, though the saga of Jackson hadn't quite concluded. Brian joined the war, and Jackson was not one to walk away from a fight. Brian and Laney had collectively ruined Jackson's life and a day of reckoning was the only recompense. Laney's newfound strength pleased Brian, but Jackson was not impressed. He sought one thing only-revenge! Jackson found the ideal moment to capitalize on Laney's presumed weakness. Her strength had not waned in the manner Jackson thought. Victorious, she stood just shy of Brian's arrival to defend her from the evil that surged. Brian and Laney stared at the memory of the antagonist to their love. Nonetheless they stood strong, and they stood together.

THE END

"Wow that was spot on babe. Good job. You are talented I see." Stephanie rested her hand on Harvey's shoulder.

"Thanks, beautiful, I try." Harvey disguised his pride.

"No, really, good job. What inspired you to be a writer?"

"It's just another means of expressing myself." Harvey was great at short and generic answers that lacked detail.

"You should stick with it." Stephanie encouraged.

"I plan to, though piano is way more important." Harvey said as he repositioned himself on the bed.

"Understandably so, but I really think you should write a book someday."

"It's funny you should mention that. I've been seriously considering writing a romance novel."

"Why romance?"

"I don't know, I am naturally romantic so the words and story should come easy." Harvey shrugged his shoulders and spoke with a confident tone.

"Well why haven't I seen this romantic side?" Stephanie revived her dormant sarcasm. She lightly tapped the side of Harvey's head.

"You want to play fight?" Harvey moved a few inches towards Stephanie, smiled then stopped. "Anyways, don't worry you will." Harvey assured.

"I will hold you to it handsome." Stephanie smiled and nodded her head as she delivered her promise.

"No need!" Harvey smiled, "I've already got some ideas."

"I like that you're romantic." Stephanie smiled as she laid her head on Harvey's shoulder.

"I look forward to treating you to my romantic side." Harvey put his arm around Stephanie and turned his head slightly, kissing her forehead.

"If it's anything like your intimacy then I am definitely ready to experience whenever you are ready to show me." Stephanie said sweetly and rather innocently given the nature of her words.

"I guess I better get moving huh?" It was Harvey's turn to tease.

"Ah something like that." Stephanie smirked.

Harvey and Stephanie laughed the night away until they fell asleep. Harvey awoke, startled that he had fallen asleep at Stephanie's house. He was pleased to wake up and find Stephanie there in his arms. He hurried out of bed and began getting dressed, "Four o'clock in the morning!" He said as he shook his head in disbelief. Amid Harvey moving about Stephanie woke up. Still groggy she said, "Just stay babe, it will be nice." She barely opened her eyes.

"What time will your kids be home in the morning?" Harvey asked.

"They are coming at 8:30!" She sat up briefly, then fell back onto the bed.

"Okay babe I'll stay then."

Harvey and Stephanie kissed for a short while then cuddled up together and fell back to sleep. The night was serene as both had what they wanted.

They were startled by a knock on the door. Stephanie rolled over and checked the alarm clock by her bed.

"What time is it?" Harvey asked.

"It's only 7:30!" Stephanie said, "Who would be at my door this early?" Stephanie spoke with an upset tone.

"Yeah, I thought you said 8:30."

"That's what mom and I originally said." Stephanie replied, worried her children would find Harvey at the house.

"I guess you'd better get the door." Harvey said.

"You're right!" Stephanie said as she put on her pajamas and headed for the bedroom door.

"Mommy!" Ariana and Johnathan yelled.

"Oh no!" Stephanie thought, "They were not supposed to be here until eight-thirty."

Stephanie opened the door. The kids gave Stephanie a huge hug.

"Mom, I thought you were bringing them at 8:30."

"Sorry Stephie, I tried to call, but your phone was going straight to voicemail."

"Oh gosh I forgot to charge it last night. Sorry, well are you stopping in, or do you have to run?" Stephanie asked, hoping that her mother had not planned to stop in.

"I have to get going, but we should do lunch or dinner soon."

"Yes, we should. I have a few things to tell you."

"I cannot wait to hear it. Sounds like it may be good news."

"It is good news mom. Okay hey I love you mom and we will get together soon." Stephanie covertly rushed her mom away.

"Okay hun, I love you too. Hey, your father says he loves you."

"Okay tell him I am looking forward to seeing him soon also." Stephanie responded.

"Okay Stephie call me this week."

"I will, bye mom, I love you." Once the door closed, Stephanie breathed a sigh of relief.

"Bye Stephie, I love you too."

Stephanie quickly helped the kids settle back in. She paced as she wondered what to do about Harvey.

"Hey there Ariana and Johnathan, it's nice to see you guys!" Harvey said with a huge smile on his face as he moved quickly down the stairs.

"Oh my, what is he doing?" Stephanie thought.

"Hey Mr. Harvey, what are you doing here?" Ariana asked. Little Johnathan just looked at Harvey and grinned.

"Nothing much. I was just discussing your piano lessons with mommy and just getting to know more about who she is. Hmm, let me see, does someone have a birthday coming up soon?" Harvey poked Ariana's arm and smiled.

"Yep, I do. I do Mr. Harvey." Johnathan smiled at his older sister's excitement.

"Guess what?" Harvey asked.

"What Mr. Harvey?" Ariana responded excitedly.

"I will be at your party!" Harvey kneeled to be eye to eye with Ariana.

"Awesome!" Ariana jumped once.

"How old will you be?" Harvey asked.

"I will be six Mr. Harvey!"

"16?"

"No!" Ariana laughed, "I will be six!" She continued.

"Okay got it, 60?" Harvey looked surprised as he fell on his back.

"Mr. Harvey you're silly. I will be six!" Ariana repeated herself. "Six."

"Oh, you will be six hun..." Harvey continued, only to soon be interrupted.

"Stop Mr. Harvey, I will be six. Mommy!" Ariana called out in frustration.

"Okay six it is then." Harvey smiled.

"Why were you and mommy talking about my piano lesson?" Ariana asked.

"Can I tell you at our next lesson?"

"Sure Mr. Harvey, sure." Ariana nodded and smiled.

"I am looking forward to our next lesson." Harvey told Ariana.

"I am too. Will you be at my party?" Ariana asked.

Harvey looked at Stephanie, "Do you want him to come?" Stephanie asked Ariana.

"Yes, mommy I want Mr. Harvey to come..."

"Ooh I want come!" Little Johnathan interrupted with broken two-year-old language.

"Duh, you will be there. You're my little brother because I'm bigger than you."

Stephanie smiled, "Be nice to your brother. Yes of course, you'll be there Johnathan and Mr. Harvey too." Harvey and Stephanie smiled at each other. It was clear that love had filled the room.

"You better be there little Johnny boy!" Harvey laughed as he picked Johnathan up briefly.

The party would be Saturday, exactly one week from the present day. The upcoming week would go rather quickly. Perhaps the old cliché rang true, 'time flies when you're having fun." Stephanie and Harvey talked often. They were naturally falling for each other. And with total security they fell. Stephanie did not know when she would smile again after Jeffery's untimely death. Harvey did not know if or when he could love again after Andrea's secret and painful betrayal.

For Harvey, 'the truth shall set you free' was a cliché that held no certainty. It had been a couple of years or more since Andrea unveiled her secret and he was yet to be set free. He thought he would always feel somewhat bound by that hurtful secret and revelation, but Stephanie made it easier to love again, and to trust again. He looked forward to Ariana's party because he would get to meet more of Stephanie's family. Being liked by her family was important to him. The time had come.

CHAPTER 19

The day of Ariana's party arrived, and the kids ran wild; the adults talked about everything from world news, sports to the joys and woes of child rearing.

Harvey got along well with all Stephanie's friends and family. He was curious about her connection to one guy.

Stephanie pulled Julie aside and asked the polarizing question- "Why is he here?"

"Girl, I brought Brian because he said he just wanted to be near you again but promised not to make any advances." Julie smirked as if she had done nothing offensive.

"Are you stupid or just plain rude? I thought you were my friend!"

"What are you talking about Stephanie?" Julie asked confused.

"You know that I have a boyfriend." Stephanie crossed her arms and spoke directly.

"It's really not that big of a deal Stephanie."

"Well, he's here, and it is a big deal Julie because you know he's interested in me." Stephanie put her hands up, landed them on her hips then cocked slightly to the right.

"What can Harvey do that Brian cannot?" Julie asked.

"Um be my boyfriend!" Stephanie offered the simplest and most logical response.

Julie shook her head.

"What is your problem anyways Julie? This is very irresponsible"

"I don't know what has gotten into me Stephanie, I am sorry." Julie said as she buried her head in shame.

"Alright, please do not let anything like this happen again though." Stephanie forgave Julie's offense.

"I will not. It was wrong of me to bring him along. I must warn you though, the guy is very persistent."

"Oh, I know how to stop guys like him." Stephanie said confidently.

"How?" Julie asked.

"Ignore them!" Stephanie responded.

"That doesn't work with Brian."

"Then why don't you date him?"

"I could never date one of my brother's friends, plus I know this guy is a player. He is seriously like a brother to me."

"You're not gaining any points. Please tell him I have a boyfriend and I am NOT interested in him." Stephanie paused momentarily, "I am serious Julie!" She continued.

"I will!" Julie promised.

"Thank you."

"You're welcome, it's the least I can do bestie."

Stephanie and Julie embraced.

The hustle and bustle of the party continued. The kids ran about freely. The adults were exhausted from the chase. There were lollipops, sugar powder mixes, donuts and pizza, apple cider and little huggies juice at the party. There were balloons and a blow-up bounce house for the children's enjoyment. There was yelling and lectures about safety from multiple adults. There were adult conversations and children's conversations just the same. The kids were having fun and that's what counted, though deeper devils joined the party.

"Brian you've got to stop this. You cannot get every girl you want, and she has a boyfriend." Julie told Brian.

"Come on sister from another mister, I have a good feeling about this."

"What are you going to do? Make her leave her boyfriend or something?" Julie laughed and shook her head.

"Precisely!" Brian said with confidence and conviction.

"Brian don't do it." Julie begged.

"Listen little sis, I am filthy rich at only 29, I actually treat women with respect; I am pretty awesome in bed so wherever I lack can be accommodated for."

"And what about Harvey?" Julie asked with a hard tone that demonstrated her anger and disagreement with Brian's intended actions. Further, she was upset about the role that she played in what could be about to potentially transpire.

"Who?" Brian asked.

"Harvey? Uh her boyfriend?" Julie explained and squealed a little.

"Oh yeah that dude! Well, I guess I can apologize in advance for his loss." Brian's arrogance did not attenuate one iota.

"Do you ever think about what he might do?" Julie asked the question Brian had not yet given adequate thought to.

"Nah, but it's not like the guy is a murderer or something."

"Brian you're playing with fire, and you know what they say…"

"No, I do not, but please enlighten me." Brian had developed a habit for portraying ignorance.

"To put it plainly if you play with fire long enough, eventually you get burned."

"I appreciate your worrying, but I can handle myself!" Brian appeared slightly offended.

"And what about Stephanie and her kids, Brian?" Julie asked.

"Listen I do not know, but there is something that I do know."

"What do you know Brian?"

"That I want this girl, and not just for fun or to bang or whatever." Brian clearly spelled out his intentions.

"You're being very selfish, and I have a very bad feeling about your decision." Julie shook her head.

"Then you can just sit back and watch how everything falls into place." Brian gave thumbs up and walked away.

Stephanie was upset that Julie brought Brian to her house without asking first. She was cleaning a bit and feeling somewhat overwhelmed, "I will be there shortly sweetie!" Harvey yelled from the back deck while talking to Stephanie's mother, Louise.

"Okay handsome I will be in the kitchen whenever you are ready."

Stephanie said, relieved that help would be on the way.

"Okay here I am!" The unwelcomed voice emanated from behind her.

"Brian, leave me alone." Stephanie said after turning around.

"How can you tell me to leave you alone before even getting to know me?" Brian asked while looking to see if Harvey was on the way yet.

"Because typically girls with boyfriends do not get to know other men."

"Well sexy, maybe our situation isn't all that typical." Brian tried another avenue to get to Stephanie.

"We do not have a situation, now please stop bothering me." Stephanie's face fueled with rage.

"Well, it doesn't mean we can't have a situation." Brian's efforts persisted.

"Okay maybe this will help, 'we cannot', now go away." Stephanie looked Brian directly in his eyes, crossed her arms and retained the enraged look upon her face.

Harvey looked on from the back deck as Stephanie and this unfamiliar guy were having a conversation. Harvey felt a little uneasy but wasn't sure how to respond or if he should just react.

"You're a female, you do not mean that. You're much more emotional than logical, but logically I am simply better for you. That's all." Brian said.

"Okay I need..." Stephanie began.

"Hey hun is everything all right?" Harvey asked with the 'overprotective boyfriend' look on his face.

"Yes, Brian was just leaving."

"Okay hey man, nice to meet you, I'm Brian!" Brian extended his hand out to Harvey.

"Yeah...Harvey!" Harvey said as he extended his hand.

Stephanie observed in disgust. It was the forbidden handshake. This was the door never meant to open. The introduction was the implicit deal made with the wrong devil. This handshake would inevitably invite darkness to join brighter days. This exchange would be the solicitation for evil to surge, to dwell among the good, the happy, the loved, and the united. The cohabitating of souls and emotions would present life's greatest dilemmas.

"I was just leaving." Bye Stephanie! Nice to...meet you, Harvey." Brian said before turning to walk away.

"Likewise!" Harvey responded.

There was a brief pause as Brian exited the kitchen. "That guy is pretty weird."

"You're telling me?"

"How do you know him, what's his name again?"

"His name is Brian and I really do not know him at all. He's Julie's friend."

"Is there something you need to tell me?" Harvey closed his eyes as he quickly remembered the pain felt when Andrea broke his heart.

"No hun there is not!" Stephanie smiled, then kissed Harvey softly on the lips."

"Okay beautiful well let me help you get this all cleaned up so you can say bye to all your guests." Harvey said as he reached for a dish that needed to be put away.

"Thank you for being so sweet Harvey."

"You're welcome, babe. It's my pleasure to please you." Harvey winked at Stephanie, then lightly rubbed her back.

"Hmm little play on words...I like!" Stephanie said jokingly as she wiped whipped vanilla frosting on Harvey's lips.

"You're going to get that off right?" Harvey smiled.

Stephanie began her attempt to remove the whipped vanilla frosting when Harvey suddenly pulled her in and began passionately and sensually kissing. They both enjoyed it. Stephanie, laughing said, "Stop it, my parents are right outside. But hey we can have dessert later." She presented that naughty look Harvey loved-Her pupils shrunk, her head tilted downward, her hands met her hip, and her butt swung a little to the left.

"Dessert later sounds perfect. Yeah, Stephanie get to cleaning, we have guests here." Harvey waved her off as he made an attempt at humor.

"We?" Stephanie returned the sarcasm.

"Yes 'we'!"

"Whatever, ha! Let's get this all cleaned up. My dessert is already heating up for you." The sexual tension continued to build. Stephanie may have been described by Jeffery as a "lady in the streets and freak in the sheets."

"Okay I am going to clean faster than I've ever cleaned a day in my life." Harvey laughed and began moving at an increased rate of speed.

The two of them chuckled as they cleaned, and it was yet another almost perfect moment. They said their goodbyes to all the guests then decided to recharge themselves before moving fully into their plans for the evening. They made their way to the living room.

"Did you have fun baby?" Stephanie asked Ariana.

"I did mommy, I did. Thank you." Ariana stared up at her mother.

"How about you Johnathan?" Stephanie asked as she knelt to be closer to Johnathan's height.

"Yes, mommy I loved bouncing and playing with all the kids." Johnathan said in broken English.

"I loved playing with all the kids too mommy." Ariana, the still energetic six-year-old said as she bounced around like the party had just begun.

"Yes, I could tell. You were so loud, which I think was adorable and it showed just how much fun you were having." Stephanie lightly pinched and shook Ariana's cheek.

"Mommy!" Ariana said in an elongated manner. "Do not shake my cheek!" Ariana paused, "So what else are we going to do tonight?"

Stephanie jokingly mushed Ariana's face.

"Mommy stopppp!" Ariana vigorously shook her head.

Stephanie laughed, "What about watching a movie together? Then you guys are going to bed."

"What movie mommy?" Ariana was always excited to spend time with her family.

"Yeah, what movie?" Johnathan joined in.

Harvey just listened in admiration at the family's interaction. "I could get used to this", he thought.

"What about *Unfrozen*?" Stephanie suggested. Her voice raised an octave in hopes of employing the power of suggestibility upon rather impressionable minds.

"Yeah mommy, yeah!' Johnathan jumped up and down.

"Ohhhh yessss, I love *Unfrozen*." Ariana said.

"Are you okay with that Harvey?" Stephanie asked.

"Please say yes Mr. Harvey, please say yes." Ariana ran over to Harvey and gripped his hands.

"Okay...yes!" Harvey smiled and made a fake attempt to tackle Ariana then run over to Johnathan.

"Oh Harvey, mom I totally seen you guys kissing earlier." Ariana broke the ice in an unexpected manner.

"Oops!" Harvey said as he covered his mouth and looked at Stephanie.

"Yeah, oops! Ariana we will talk about that later." Stephanie diverted attention away from the somewhat awkward subject.

215

"Okay mommy, I liked seeing you and Mr. Harvey together though." Ariana apparently was not done delivering surprises.

"Oh..." Stephanie said surprised and at a loss for words. She smiled at the words which put her more at ease about the relationship with Harvey and bringing him into the kids' lives.

The moment was perfect, and the mood was precisely what they needed. Harvey's connection to the children was natural and the way to a woman's heart was through her kids. And well, Harvey had found his way into Stephanie's heart. They'd only been dating a short while, but their growth was impeccable; there was certainly better to come. There was such a peace and natural joy about their relationship.

The movie concluded and Stephanie put the kids to bed. She loved being with her kids, but now it was time for Harvey and her to spend some much needed, and highly anticipated time alone.

"I've been waiting for this all night long!" Stephanie said as she led Harvey to the bedroom where they would spend the night. "Are you ready?"

"The question is, are you ready?" Harvey asked as he turned down the lights.

CHAPTER 20

They laid in darkness, whispering sweet nothings and touching politely. Harvey slipped his hands down Stephanie's pants, and she whispered his name. Their passion moved into overdrive. Their longing for each other was unexplainable. Harvey kissed and licked Stephanie's neck as she touched him everywhere imaginable. He groaned as to demonstrate how remarkable her touches felt.

"Screw me Harvey, right now." Stephanie said as she excited Harvey more by talking dirty-ish and licking him in sensual areas.
"Don't you worry beautiful, I will!"

Harvey licked all the way down Stephanie's body stopping in between her legs. He looked up at her and marveled at the magic they'd created. He could only see a miniscule representation of her enjoyment because he was relying on minimal light shining in from outside her bedroom window. He slowly slid his tongue out of his mouth, then into her once forbidden hole. She moaned and moaned until she pulled Harvey up and said, "Fuck me, Harvey!"

He inserted himself inside of Stephanie and it happened, their souls connected from that moment on and forever. Love took on new meaning as their emotions would now be guided by feelings of false security. Healthy and unhealthy possessiveness was on the horizon. Jealousy would arise as a primary fire to dampen. There was much to be harvested. Harvey and Stephanie hoped not to water the wrong plants.

The next three months reaffirmed that no relationship went without chaos and problems.

"Why are you always on your phone Harvey?" Stephanie would often ask.
"Am I not allowed to talk to friends or family?"
"Why don't you ever show me?" Stephanie asked.
"You really spend too much time worrying about my phone.
"It makes it seem like you have something to hide." She would lean over

his shoulder and try to see who he was talking to.

"You know what? Here!" Harvey would sometimes toss his phone to Stephanie. "Look as long as you want since you're so obsessed over my freaking phone." That was the typical response.

"Thanks, I will!" Stephanie replied. She would never find anything, but, looking exonerated Harvey and offered security for Stephanie.

That was just one of many arguments that would occur.

"Why do you insist on wearing those tight-fitted outfits?" Harvey would ask, usually in relation to what Stephanie chose to wear to work.

"Because I like the outfit, Harvey."

"Whatever happened to, 'for your eyes only'?" Harvey would ask in a dark tone.

"Oh my-gosh, nobody cares. It's just an outfit."

"You just do not understand." Harvey genuinely wished Stephanie could see the world through his eyes for once.

"Nope sorry, I do not."

Sometimes Stephanie would begrudgingly change her outfit. While other times she would wear provocative outfits simply to upset Harvey.

Against better judgment, she let Harvey move in which opened the door for more problems.

"Something has been bothering me..." Stephanie's predictable introduction always caused Harvey's blood to boil.

"Okay what is it?"

"Would you please mop as well when you clean the house?"

"Oh, geez I don't know. Can you try saying thank you when I do clean the house?"

"You should help whether I say thank you or not. I cook every day, don't I?" Stephanie yelled and stomped her feet. The reality is no one compared to Jeffery. Dating Harvey reminded Stephanie of how much she longed for Jeffery.

"And I clean every day you ungrateful...ugh!" Harvey would frequently attempt to walk away.

"You know I can care less if you call me hurtful names."

"You seriously need help. All you want to do is argue."

"No, I just want you to clean the house the way I would."

"Have fun with that. You want to know why?"

"Why, Mr. Know-it-All?"

"Because for the last...time, I...AM...NOT...YOU!" Harvey spoke loudly but tried maintaining an acceptable decorum of speech when speaking to another adult.

"That's clear!" Stephanie would further insult Harvey. "I do not want my children to hear us fighting like this..." Stephanie softened after a brief pause.

"I'm going to the gym. I will be back in a couple of hours."

"Fine, leave. You always run away when we argue." Stephanie said in a dejected tone of voice.

"Exactly, I'd rather run than continue fighting with you; you will never stop."

"Fine I will stop. Just don't leave."

"Dude, what the heck is your problem? I need to go to the gym to clear my head."

"What do you mean baby?" Stephanie would then ask in a sweet voice as if an argument had not just happened.

"You argue, you yell, you insult, you tell me to leave then you show a façade of sweetness and tell me not to leave. My brain does not understand you anymore." Harvey had learned how to appropriately summarize what was going on between them.

At the end of this argument Stephanie held her head and was almost in tears. She was embarrassed at how she'd been acting lately. They would love strong, fight hard, then make up. Love had a way of winning, but for everyone there are non-negotiables that yield points of no return. Harvey knew his, but Stephanie did not know hers.

The next several days were wonderful between Harvey and Stephanie. The family laughed often through board games, enjoyed time at the beach and other outdoor activities under the brightly shining sun. While at the beach, Stephanie and some guy locked eyes for a moment in time and it triggered a fear and an anger in Harvey like he had never felt as strongly until now.

The argument of all arguments ensued then exploded. Harvey yelled the words which impacted by every fiber of Stephanie's being, "Jeffery probably committed suicide just to get away from you!" Harvey delivered the blow from which recovery would likely be impossible.

Stephanie stopped whatever she was saying. She could not believe the words she'd just heard. Jeffery was the amazing love of her life and the father of her lovely children. "How could he say...that?" She questioned within herself. She took a deep breath then sat down to fully process what had just transpired.

Harvey repeatedly apologized, but what he just said would pave the way for irreparable destruction, both collateral and otherwise.

"I have to get away from you. I'm going to Julies."

"Babe please don't leave like this. I am so sorry." Harvey said while softly grabbing Stephanie's hand.

Stephanie held her head low and gently removed her hand from Harvey's. "I will see you tonight." Stephanie dropped tears and Harvey's heart broke.

Stephanie called Julie, "Hey can I come over?"

"Steph, you know you are welcomed at my house anytime. You don't even have to ask."

"Thanks bestie, I know."

"Okay, Stephanie what's wrong?"

"Nothing, it's nothing." Stephanie said quickly.

"I can hear the sadness in your voice."

"I'll tell you about it when I get there." Stephanie choked back a few tears then cleared her throat. She hung up the phone and yelled for the kids to come downstairs.

Stephanie and the kids arrived at Julie's and as always were welcomed with open arms.

"Girl what happened?" Julie asked.

"Harvey said something I...we may never recover from." Stephanie shook her head.

"What did he say?" Julie was genuinely concerned.

"I cannot...Just can't even repeat it. This is the first time that I can say he legitimately hurt my heart." Stephanie fought back tears.

"I am sorry, and you know that I am always available to talk if you ever need to. Girl, you know that you and the kids are always welcomed here."

"Thank you. I really appreciate you being such a great friend." Stephanie responded barely lifting her head.

"Of course. You don't even have to ask, just show up."

"Hey, aren't you that Stephanie girl?" Brian asked.

"Brian seriously I understand being persistent but leave the poor girl alone." Julie interjected.

"Um ya and aren't you that Brian dude?" Stephanie surprised both Brian and Julie.

"Okay, okay I guess I deserved that." Brian nodded.

"You did!" Stephanie laughed lightly to hide the tears.

"So how have you been?" Brian asked, making small talk.

"I have been all right, how about you?"

"Honestly, I've been great. Very busy with my business, but can I just be honest about something?" Brian said as he moved in slightly closer.

"Of course, you can." Stephanie responded.

"I was a total loser last time and I just want to 'start over'-whatever that even means. I guess what I'm asking is can we be friends. I will not rush you or disrespect whatever relationship you have going on, but I'd really like to be your friend." Brian's eyes spoke to the sincerity of the words that had just emanated from his lips.

"Brian she's unavailable man!" Julie said trying to defend Stephanie.

"It's okay Julie. Thank you though. I accept your apology and yeah, we can be friends but seriously nothing more."

"Stephanie are you sure about this?" Julie asked.

"Why not?" Stephanie responded.

"Okay I'm out of it then." Julie responded. Julie and Brian were best friends. The three of them, her, her brother, and Brian hung out often. There was never any kind of relationship besides friendship between them.

"It's about time Julie." Brian added.

"You can give me your number Brian and I will text you sometime." Stephanie's limp and insecure body language exemplified a lack of surety about her decision.

Brian wrote his number down for Stephanie, "I really hope you contact me."

"Listen I am seeing someone, and I am not the kind of lady that cheats on her man. I'm sorry I will not be able to communicate with you!" Stephanie said in a stoic manner.

Stephanie paused, then called for the kids. "Come on guys let's go."

The kids hurried down the stairs. "Thank you both for being so sweet, but I am going to head home and try to get some sleep."

The night after the crushing statement was awkward. "How could Harvey say that Jeffery committed suicide to get away from me?"

"I wish you'd come closer babe." Harvey said.

"And I wish you'd go to the couch."

"Fine!" Harvey rolled out of bed and headed towards the couch.

Harvey paused at the door. He wished that Stephanie would ask him to stay like in times past. But she said nothing. She did not roll over; she did not look at him-she just silently wept. She was a woman scorned. Harvey knew a little something about the bible and one scripture was the bane of his existence, "Hell hath no fury like a woman scorned!" He was admittedly unprepared.

Harvey looked at Stephanie longing for her to look back at him. He was amazed by her beauty even in the dark of night. She illuminated a dark room and heated a cold heart. For the first time in a long time someone made him feel that it was safe to love again, and he hurt her; precisely what he feared she would do to him. With his words made her feel pain and as if he could no longer make her happy.

"I love you, Stephanie!"

Stephanie clenched her pillow and cried. She thought she'd finally buried Jeffery, but here he was resurrected. The hole in her heart had returned, or worse it had never been filled. Harvey was the man that filled that hole to the best of his ability, and now also the man responsible for reopening the wound.

Stephanie did not know what to do. She just cried and tried to forget Jeffery, and Harvey's decrepit words. Ariana would periodically console Stephanie as best she could. It became even sweeter when Johnathan made his journey to the room also. Stephanie held it together when the kids were in the room, though as soon as they were gone her pillow fell victim to painful tears, unsettled fears, the struggle with years past and the repressed anger bottled for far too long.

They were a unique little family. Harvey even periodically brought Ariana to play with Raina. Raina and Ariana were like two peas in a pod. They even allowed Johnathan to join. Stephanie could feel the drifting, and she had no clue how to stop it.

Harvey desperately wished he could take back what he said. He was losing her, but he wasn't ready to let go. "If only she could see my heart, feel my love and experience my pain she would come back, she would draw closer and let us heal together." Harvey thought to himself.

Hurt and saddened, Stephanie looked at Brian's number then grabbed her cell phone, "No I can't!" Stephanie rolled over and went to sleep.

Time would always serve as the uninhibited teller of truth. Truth will always be revealed in the unrestricted elements of time. The truth shall set you free; other times the truth shall just bring pain.

CHAPTER 21

Several weeks passed and the fighting continued, often about small matters magnified. Things like the way he mowed the lawn, him going for walks without telling her where he was going and when he would be returning. They fought about the outfits that the other wore. Harvey felt that Stephanie was judgmental and concerned with the insignificant things of life-the clothes he wore and the way he wore them, the way he brushed his hair, his car being too dirty, him being too opinionated, and her children not always being included when spent time with Raina.

He was concerned with how she wore her hair and the fitting of certain clothes. Stephanie sometimes disapproved of the way Harvey spoke to her children, and he would usually respond with, "It's not my fault you'd rather be your children's friend rather than their parent."

"Do not tell me how to raise 'my' kids!"

Harvey was close with Ariana but did not care much for Johnathan; deep inside Harvey felt Johnathan was irritating and difficult. He often viewed the boy as a brat. Nevertheless, Harvey attempted to build a relationship with Johnathan anyway. He would frequently try splitting his mother and Harvey-attempting to turn one against the other.

"Mommy, Harvey is yelling at me!" Johnathan would say.

"Harvey, I have asked you not to yell at my child." Stephanie would typically quickly come to Johnathan's defense.

"Stephanie, really? You should be pulling me aside and discussing this in private. You don't even know what happened."

"I do not need to know what happened!"

"I do not have time for this. That is the most ridiculous thing I've ever heard." Harvey would sometimes respond.

"Do what you always do-walk away!" Stephanie's usual response when Harvey turned his back to her.

"That's because you're totally irrational when it comes to your kids." Harvey would turn back around and explain why he removes himself from the situation.

"That's why they're my kids."

"Okay this time I am really walking away." Harvey would shake his head to show that he had officially heard enough.

"Good!" Stephanie would deliver the final stab to the argument.

After so much arguing Harvey found comfort in what he knew best - the piano. He sat there, but his mind and fingers were not on one accord. The relationship was draining him. He loved Stephanie but could sense he was losing her. He didn't know how to alter their course. He turned from the piano and looked at Stephanie. She had no idea that he was watching. She was texting and smiling more than Harvey had seen in a long time. Then she would occasionally look up to see if Harvey was watching. Harvey's intuition told him what he did not want to believe-That she had begun getting to know another man.

"Hun?" Harvey called out.
"Yeah babe?" Stephanie responded.
"Can I ask you a question?"
"You can ask me anything."
"Just be totally honest with me okay." Was Harvey's request. He took a deep breath in preparation for the difficult question.
"Okay!"
"Are you moving on?" Harvey asked.

"No Harvey I would never do that to you."

"Why does my gut feeling tell me that you are?" Harvey asked as he tried looking at Stephanie's eyes and body language.

"Harvey you are always getting these intuitive types of feelings or thoughts, and they're just wrong!" Stephanie said confidently.

"Well, men can have intuition as well."

"Well, you need to stop worrying so much!"

"Worry is sometimes based on perceived fears or faulty perceptions, but sometimes worry is a legitimate way of telling someone that something is wrong."

"Harvey nothing is wrong so just stop your worrying!" Stephanie said in a frustrated tone.

"Why do you always dismiss my feelings?"

"Because they're stupid Harvey. That's why!"

"Never mind, go back to your texting. I am going to sit here at this piano where you used to join me and smile as I played for you. I guess whoever you're texting is more important though." Harvey said as he shook his head and walked away.

Stephanie felt like the worst girlfriend. She came and sat with Harvey as he serenaded her with graceful piano sounds. Her smiles lacked authenticity. Her interest lacked depth. Her presence lacked genuineness. Harvey could sense the detachment and deficiency between them. Their relationship and their love were both becoming an anomaly. Harvey yearned a state of normalcy, but the climb presented as too great, and commitment was vanishing. Stephanie sat for a little while longer then went to prepare dinner. Occasionally Harvey would turn to look at Stephanie. He wanted to see love in her eyes, to know that she still desired all of him and to offer all of herself; all his heart could sense was absence. His mind foretold tears and great pain. Harvey hoped she would look at him, but she continued cooking and texting. For the first time Harvey felt he no longer mattered and that his presence was of minimal importance.

"Harvey, kids, dinner is done!" Stephanie yelled.

Harvey's mind had discarded compartmentalization. He was overwhelmed, "You guys eat. I am going to play a few songs."

"Mr. Harvey we always eat together!" Ariana said with much sadness in her voice.

Harvey got up and walked towards the table. He bent down and kissed Ariana's forehead, "Maybe tomorrow pretty girl!" Harvey's eyes filled with water.
"Whatever." Stephanie muttered.

Ariana watched teary-eyed as Harvey walked back to the piano. He played and sang three songs-*All of Me* by John Legend, *It Will Rain* by Bruno Mars, and *Amazing Grace (Broken Vessels)* by Hillsong United.

All Of Me

What would I do without your smart mouth
Drawing me in, and you kicking me out
Got my head spinning, no kidding, I can't pin you down
What's going on in that beautiful mind
I'm on your magical mystery ride
And I'm so dizzy, don't know what hit me, but I will be alright

My head's under water
But I'm breathing fine
You're crazy and I'm out of my mind

'Cause all me
Loves all you
Love your curves and all your edges
All your perfect imperfections
Give your all to me
I will give my all to you
You're my end and my beginning
Even when I lose I'm winning
'Cause I give you all, of me
And you give me all, of you

How many times do I have to tell you
Even when you're crying you're beautiful
too
The world is beating you down, I'm around
through every mood
You're my downfall, you're my muse
My worst distraction, my rhythm and
blues
I can't stop singing, it's ringing, in my head
for you

My head's under water
But I'm breathing fine
You're crazy and I'm out of my mind

'Cause all me
Loves all you
Love your curves and all your edges
All your perfect imperfections
Give your all to me
I will give my all to you
You're my end and my beginning

237

Even when I lose I'm winning
'Cause I give you all, of me
And you give me all, of you

Cards on the table, we're both showing
hearts
Risking it all, though it's hard

'Cause all me
Loves all you
Love your curves and all your edges
All your perfect imperfections
Give your all to me
I will give my all to you
You're my end and my beginning
Even when I lose I'm winning
'Cause I give you all me
And you give me all you

I give you all, all me
And you give me all, all you

Harvey wanted all of Stephanie: her heart, her mind, her body and her love. He knew she wasn't perfect, but he was ready and willing to accept her for exactly who she was. He was ready to risk it all to experience the greatness that love had to offer. He knew it wouldn't be easy, but she was who he wanted.

Harvey took a deep breath and moved on to the next song.

It Will Rain

If you ever leave me, baby,
Leave some morphine at my door
'Cause it would take a whole lot of
medication
To realize what we used to have,
We don't have it anymore.

There's no religion that could save me
No matter how long my knees are on the
floor
So keep in mind all the sacrifices I'm makin'
To keep you by my side
To keep you from walkin' out the door.

'Cause there'll be no sunlight
If I lose you, baby
There'll be no clear skies
If I lose you, baby
Just like the clouds
My eyes will do the same, if you walk
away
Everyday it'll rain, rain, ra-a-a-ain

I will never be your mother's favorite
Your daddy can't even look me in the eye
Ooh, if I was in their shoes, I'd be doing the
same thing
Sayin' "There goes my little girl
Walkin' with that troublesome guy"
But they're just afraid of something they
can't understand

Ooh, but little darlin' watch me change their minds
Yeah for you I will try I will try I will try I will try
I will pick up these broken pieces 'til I'm bleeding
If that'll make you mine

'Cause there'll be no sunlight
If I lose you, baby
There'll be no clear skies
If I lose you, baby
Just like the clouds
My eyes will do the same, if you walk away
Everyday it'll rain, rain, ra-a-a-ain

Oh, don't you say (don't you say) goodbye (goodbye),
Don't you say (don't you say) goodbye (goodbye)
I will pick up these broken pieces 'til I'm bleeding
If that'll make it right

'Cause there'll be no sunlight
If I lose you, baby
There'll be no clear skies
If I lose you, baby
Just like the clouds
My eyes will do the same, if you walk away
Everyday it'll rain, rain, ra-a-a-ain.

One of Harvey's worst fears was losing Stephanie. He didn't think she truly understood how dangerously he loved her. The thought of losing her made him sick. She was often the reason he smiled, amongst other things. Harvey wasn't ready to hurt again, though he could see pain in the distant decreasing time and space. She was his sunlight and his brighter day. Stephanie had been his protection from tears.

He no longer operated behind the blinding veil of love. He could sense their relationship was failing, and that it was most likely, though not proven, due to Stephanie getting to know another man. Their relationship was becoming increasingly broken. He felt Stephanie still loved him, but he could sense something was wrong.

He began playing and singing one of his mother's favorite songs by Hillsong.

Amazing Grace (Broken Vessels)

All these pieces
Broken and shattered
In mercy gathered
Mended and whole
Empty handed
But not forsaken
I've been set free

I've been set free

Amazing grace
How sweet the sound
That saved a wretch like me
I once was lost
But now I'm found
Was blind but now I see

Oh I can see You know
Oh I can see the love in Your eyes
Laying Yourself down
Raising up the broken to life

You take our failure
You take our weakness
You set Your treasure
In jars of clay
So take this heart Lord
I will be your vessel
The world to see
Your life in me

Harvey took a deep breath and repeated the course. He thought about the words, "Was blind, but now I see..." It was those lyrics that lead to him confronting Stephanie.

"Okay, I'm not blind Stephanie! What's...his...name?" Harvey demanded.

"Can we not do this in front of the kids?" Stephanie pleaded.

"Can you not text him in front of the kids?" Harvey offered a similar solution.

"Listen as soon as they go to their room we will talk, but I'm not texting a guy. I do not know why you are so worried." Stephanie folded her arms.

Harvey walked outside to the back deck to compose himself in preparation for the conversation to come. After a few moments Stephanie joined him.

"Okay so what is your problem, Harvey?" Stephanie stood with her hands on her hips.

"What's my problem?"

"Uh yeah?"

"My problem is that I think you are texting someone else. I think you are getting to know another guy, and I want the truth from you." Harvey moved a little closer to Stephanie.

"Harvey I am not talking to another guy!" Stephanie maintained her original position.

"Okay then why don't you prove it?" Harvey suggested.

"How can I prove that, Harvey?"

"Let me go through your call log and text messages."

"Um no that's just creepy!"

"You know in healthy relationships there are no secrets!" Harvey looked at Stephanie.

"Well, I am not letting you see my phone."

"And that's because you have something to hide."

"No, I do not!" Stephanie responded with fury and frustration.

"Then why won't you let me see your phone?"

"Because I do not want to." Stephanie offered a simple response.

"I will trust my gut feeling then!" Harvey nodded and began walking away.

"Trust what you want, I am going to bed." Stephanie responded.

Harvey turned around briefly, "Whatever!" Harvey waved Stephanie away, turned then kept walking.

Things were not improving. Stephanie remained distant, the relationship continued to be more of a strain than a joy and Harvey held strong to the belief his girlfriend was being unfaithful.

The day came when, quote on quote, Stephanie had had enough. "I am going out with Julie!"

"Why didn't you tell me this sooner?"

"I am sorry. It was planned last minute. It's just a girls' night babe!" Stephanie responded.

"Okay well can you please let me know ahead of time from now on?" Harvey asked.

"I definitely will." Stephanie would have said anything to get out of there.

Stephanie got in the shower then got dressed. Harvey was concerned because of how amazing she looked. He wanted to ask her if she was really going to see another guy but lacked the strength to confront her.

"Alright I will see you tonight." Stephanie said as she moved in for a light kiss.

"Around what time?" Harvey asked.

"Um I am not sure, but I will text you when I have a better idea as to when I will be home."

"Okay well I will see you later."

Stephanie left and Harvey tried to focus on something different than his belief that his girlfriend was cheating on him.

"All right kids how about we go to the store to get some popcorn for the awesome movies we are going to watch while your mother is gone." Harvey tried to remain positive.

"Yay let's go right now!" Ariana said.

Johnathan jumped for excitement as well.

"Why didn't you go out with mommy?" Johnathan asked.

"I wish I had the answer, but I do not know Johnathan." Harvey said quickly.

"Don't be silly, it's because mommy went out with another friend." Ariana said in a matter-of-fact manner.

"Shall we go now?" Harvey said.

"Yes!" The children yelled simultaneously.

Harvey and the kids fell asleep watching the movie. Stephanie was out later than Harvey hoped she would be. Stephanie parked in front of a different house and called Brian, per se.

"Hey Brian!" Stephanie said.

"Hey there beautiful." Brian responded.

"I know that it was only our first date, but I really think it went very well." Stephanie informed Brian.

"I totally agree beautiful, and I would like to see you again." Brian said.

"I think I could make that happen."

"When is good for you?" Brian asked. He always tried being the perfect gentleman, despite his disregard for the feelings of other men.

"Two weeks, Saturday would be great."

"It's a date. I will plan something wonderful for us." Brian assured Stephanie.

"I know you will handsome."

"I enjoyed tonight as well though."

"I really liked you teaching me golf, and the art museum was really nice as well." Stephanie smiled.

"Are you home yet?"

"Yes, but I think the kids are sleeping so I am just outside talking to you." Stephanie said as she looked inside of the house to check for any signs of movement.

"Shouldn't you get in there?" Brian asked.

"I will in just a moment. I just wanted to call and tell you how much I enjoyed seeing you tonight." Stephanie had begun giving her heart to another man-Harvey's greatest fear.

"I enjoyed our time together also." Brian responded.

"Thank you for an awesome night."

"You're welcome and thank you as well."

"You're welcome." Stephanie maintained her manners.

"Well..." Brian began to speak.

"I gotta get my butt in the house now, goodnight, Brian!" Stephanie interrupted.

"Goodnight Stephanie." Brian responded respectively.

Stephanie crept into the house.

Stephanie texted Julie, "Hey bestie, thanks for being the best friend a girl could have." Julie was wide awake playing cards and listening to music with some friends.

"Hey what time is it?" Stephanie asked herself as she checked her phone.

There was a dead, awkward silence. Stephanie hoped not to wake anyone.

Harvey awoke and walked downstairs.

"It is almost two o'clock in the morning Stephanie!" Harvey said groggily.

"Harvey, I have been here. I don't know what you are talking about. You fell asleep.

"Why are you on the couch?" Harvey asked.

"It is just where I felt like sleeping tonight."

"Goodnight!" Harvey said as he did not have the energy to address the matter now.

Harvey carried Ariana to her room, then returned to carry Johnathan. He slept in the bed with Stephanie that night, but wondered, "Who is this stranger beside me?"

The next two weeks produced no hope for the relationship. The passion was gone, the love was fading fast, and commitment appeared scarce. Hope was fleeting. The fight they once had was no more. That desire for better had quickly become acceptance of demise.

"I'm going out in two days!" Stephanie gave Harvey a little more notice that before.
"This Saturday?" Harvey asked.
"Yes!" Stephanie responded.
"Okay well you will need to find a babysitter because I am going to make plans as well."
"With?" Stephanie asked.
"I do not know yet, probably Larry!"
"That guy is such a freaking loser."
"Do you always have to criticize everyone?"

"If I think they deserve it."
Stephanie's attitude towards Harvey was worsening.

"I guess just be who you are!"
Harvey attempted to end the conversation.

"I will, thank you!" Stephanie responded sarcastically.

"Do you want to go for a walk or something?" Harvey asked.

"Sure!" Stephanie decided to oblige.

Harvey and Stephanie walked and talked. They occasionally held hands and presented their best smile. The saddest element about the road to ruin was that the road to redemption was plausible.

The time had come, and it was respectively another day that could change everything. The value of a moment would be forever lost until it surfaced as a memory. We have the power to choose, but without wisdom power leads to hurt, disappointment, danger, and ruin. Stephanie chose the road to ruin; Harvey could not walk the road to redemption alone. He knew Larry would offer sound advice. However, the storm awaiting at home reeked of ambiguity. The more complexed question was - Who would be returning to him?

CHAPTER 22

Harvey returned home from hanging out with Larry. Larry didn't seem hopeful about Harvey's relationship with Stephanie. He told Harvey it seemed like, for whatever reason Stephanie was no longer committed to the relationship or in love with him. He cautioned Harvey not to assume infidelity. Harvey posed the question, "do you think people fall out of love because they were never meant to 'fall' in love, but rather to walk in love?"

Larry agreed with Harvey about walking in love but sensed strongly that Stephanie may be emotionally moving on. He also felt it wouldn't be long before she physically moved on as well.

Harvey couldn't handle abandonment of any sort, but nonetheless it appeared inevitable. He had a feeling Stephanie would be out late. He did the unimaginable-He cried in front of his best guy friend. He wept at the thought of her in the arms of another man. He wept at the thought of her loving someone else, her lying beside another man, telling him all her woes and joys, and talking about the moments of life. He didn't want to become a topic of Stephanie's past; the guy she told the other guy about. His heart was already breaking, and she hadn't even abandoned him yet. His greatest fear was emotional hurt at the hand of a woman, yet again.

The unfortunate thing about life is we do not always control what happens to us. We can only control how we respond. Whenever Harvey was deep in thought he would close his eyes.

Unlike Harvey, Stephanie was not crying any tears. She was having the night of her life, and ultimately the night that would change everything. It would be the night she would never forget, even if she tried. This night would be the night that sealed the fate of Stephanie and Harvey's relationship.

Their night started out at the golf course.

"Are you ready to show me your swing?" Brian asked.
"Of course, cutie pie. I want to see yours also." Stephanie responded flirtatiously.

"No problem. I definitely will." Brian smiled.

"I'm sure you're pretty good at it." Stephanie smirked as she looked Brian up and down.

Brian impressed Stephanie with his ability to golf well. He watched her. She wasn't bad, but he knew it was his duty to help her hone her skills.

"Okay so you have to stand like this." Brian lightly touched Stephanie's waist.

"Okay thanks. Should I bend my knees?" Stephanie asked as she slid her butt slightly against his leg.

"Yes, slightly! And your butt should be about this high." Brian lifted Stephanie slightly.

"I really like when he touches me like that." Stephanie thought. "Should I feel guilty?"

"Hey you're quiet!" Brian pointed out as he patted Stephanie's back.

"Sorry, I was just thinking." Stephanie said in monotone voice, lacking energy.

"I hope it was about me." Brian added, attempting to liven up the mood.

"I guess you will just have to wait and see!" Stephanie smirked, while trying as best she could to mask her frustration.

There was a brief silence and Stephanie thought, "What about Harvey?" She was saddened about the apparent hurt she stood to cause.

Harvey was gentle and kind, wonderful and nice. For the moment he was her present, but now Stephanie began classifying him as a storied element of her past. Stephanie was disappointed, but selfishly she honored and preferred happiness over devout integrity. Harvey was her present and ultimately her past. She wasn't certain but felt that Brian would be the guy she would exclusively date after Harvey.

"All right pretty lady, let me see that swing." Brian said as he tapped Stephanie's hip.

"Okay here goes." Stephanie said shortly before swinging the golf club.

Brian watched Stephanie's swing, the direction and landing of the ball. "Not bad!" Brian said.

"Oh, stop it. I stink at this, and you know it!" Stephanie lowered her eyes in disappointment.

Brian erupted in laughter, "Okay yeah that was really bad!" He continued.

"Hey now!" Stephanie made her best pouty face.

"Okay I am sorry. So sorry!" Brian pretended to drop to one knee to apologize.

"Ha! Ha, it worked!"

"What worked?"

"My pouty face!" Stephanie said as she softly punched Brian's arm.

"Wow I cannot believe I fell for the oldest trick known to man." Brian shook his head.

"Indeed, mister you did." Stephanie nodded in agreement and displayed her victory on her face.

"I may have to make you pay for that later!' Brian smirked.

"Hmm how so?"

"Well, well, well I guess you will find out when it happens." Brian allowed the tension to build a bit more.

"No worries, sir!" Stephanie ran her fingers through her hair and smiled.

"Why not ma'am?"

"Because I am most definitely a patient woman."

"Patience is certainly a virtue."

"It is."

"Are you hungry?"

"I am a little hungry."

"Can I take you somewhere special?"

"Sure, but where?"

"Don't worry you will be impressed. I've thought this out pretty well." Brian pointed his right index finger and waved it up and down.

"Hmm I trust in your planning skills."

"Are you ready to go?"

"I'm ready whenever you are."

Brian and Stephanie walked back to his car. Eventually they arrived at their destination.

"Where are we?"

"Oh, I thought you were patient."

"I am!"

They approached to the door, then walked in.

"I want you to sit back and relax. Welcome to Brian's world!"

"What do you mean?"

"This is my house, Stephanie."

"Shut...the...eff...up! No, it's not!" Stephanie playfully pushed Brian.

"No, seriously it is!" Brian responded as he wrapped his arms around Stephanie's waist and pulled her in for a hug.

"I do not believe you."

"I can show you the deed and title."

"But this is like a mansion!"

"About that..." Brian paused.

"What do you mean?"

"I do not know if I want to tell you because I want you to like me and want me for the right reasons." Brian looked down while responding.

"You can tell me anything. I already like the 'you' I've come to know up to this point."

"Make yourself at home and I will be right back." Brian's right hand grazed the back of Stephanie's hair.

Stephanie sat in awe of Brian's house. The exterior walkway was a charcoal brick finish and the house matched. The roof was brown and shingled clay. The plants along the walkway added much to beautify the path. The windows were a mixture of square and oval stained-glass. The walkway was illuminated with beautiful outdoor lamps. Brian had a heated uniquely shaped pool with lights surrounding the exterior.

"Are you comfortable?" Brian asked as he returned.

"Yes, I am, thank you!"

"Want to join me in the kitchen?"

"Yes, I do, but I am not cooking."

Brian laughed as Stephanie followed him into the kitchen. "Hey where is your refrigerator?" Stephanie inquired.

Brian typed in a code on the left kitchen wall, "here it is!" The computer-programmed refrigerator slid forward as the wall covering it rose into the ceiling.

"Okay that is epically awesome! What do you do?"

"We will get to that!" Brian had become very good at building tension.

According to Stephanie, this house belonged in a magazine or television show.

She thought about Harvey but tried quickly putting him to the back of her mind.

Upon first walking into the front door there were hanging lights-some neon and some regular. The chandelier: white gold with several dangling lights and pieces. Plants were placed strategically throughout. The built-in fireplace was black with gold trim and automatic lights. The couches rotated for the entertainment on the other side of the living room. Surprisingly, the young 27-year-old possessed an antique Victorian dining room table. The trim was an Oakwood, and the floors were a mixture of hardwood and off-white ceramic tiles. The second level had a balcony overlooking the entire first level. The kitchen had an island and a built-in double wall oven encased by red brick. The hallway was akin to that of a five-star hotel. The windows provided an amazing view of the lake; the abnormal size aquarium sat beside. There was more to show, but it didn't take much to convince Stephanie that Brian's house was remarkable beyond imagination.

"So now what do you do for work?"

"I am an investment banker and I own several real estate properties."

"Very impressed mister, very impressed."

"I am in no way arrogant, nor do I think I'm better than anyone else." Brian provided the unexpected response.

They smiled during the silence that allowed for the changing of gears.

"What do you want for dinner?"

"What about haddock, rice and vegetables?" Stephanie answered quickly.

"Are you sure?"

"Yes, I am. Do you want to help me cook?"

"That could be fun."

Stephanie's phone began to ring from the living room.

"Who's calling you?"

"Hey now, you are not my boyfriend!" Stephanie responded cynically.

"Fair enough."

"Anyways let's get cooking. It's already almost eight thirty at night!" Stephanie began getting a bit restless as she did not want Harvey to start to worry too much.

"Okay let's get to it pretty lady."

They were a good team in the kitchen. Dinner was ready before long. Dinner was enjoyable-the food, the conversation, and the sum of the experience.

"Hey, do you want to watch a movie?"

"Sure, it's only about ten o'clock!"

"Do you have a curfew or something?" Brian asked through his laughter.

They sat and watched a fast-paced action movie. For a while their hands behaved, but eventually the touching began. Following the touching, kissing started. First, they were just light pecks, but Stephanie put an end to the intimacy.

"I really do not want to do this to Harvey!" She thought to herself.

Though she stopped kissing and touching she continued to lay in Brian's arms. Brian's hormones were raging, and he wanted Stephanie more than she knew. Gradually he worked up to slowly kissing her neck. She moaned, but pushed him away, "Stop Brian, not yet!"

Brian would relinquish his desires momentarily then the moment came where he slid his hand down her pants and inserted his fingers deep inside while sucking her neck. Stephanie wanted to stop him once more, but the sensation was too overwhelming. She turned and started to undress, and Brian helped her with the task at hand. He began disrobing himself. Now in his underwear they caressed private parts then the ringing of Stephanie's phone startled them to a halt.

"Stop!" Stephanie checked her phone, "Harvey!" She said to herself.

It was now 12:30 AM, "This is a problem. How can I possibly stop?" She thought.
"Is everything okay?"
Stephanie ignored him, "I have to stop." She convinced herself.
"Stephanie is everything okay?" Brian asked once more.
"I am sorry, yes, it is. I have to go though." Stephanie responded, sounding as if she was out of breath.
Stephanie put her phone down and walked towards the bed to get her clothes. Brian watched and contemplated his next

move. He, in a sexual manner pushed her towards the bed and pulled her pants down. He licked her between her legs. Every time she rose to tell him to stop, she would merely put her hand on his head and say, "Oh yeah Brian-just like that. Lick right there!"

Her window of opposition was closing. She was about to hurt Harvey and she felt powerless to stop what was brewing. Brian came up momentarily and their eyes met. It was then that they knew forbiddance was now irrelevant; what he wanted, what she feared, what she hoped to avoid - would happen.

The call went unanswered, and it was at that moment everything changed. Harvey knew something was different. He presumed his point of no return had come. He wasn't sure why or what happened, but he just knew the love he once shared with Stephanie-A woman he held dear, would soon be no more.

Stephanie felt good and horrible, elated and depressed-all at the same time. She loved Harvey, but just not enough. She wanted more, needed more and Brian was more. He was rich and handsome and funny and sweet and new. All the things that could certainly make the eighty-twenty rule applicable. She was willing to leave what she had for the possibility of something better. She could not believe she cheated on Harvey. That was never her intention, but Brian was more persistent than she expected so early on. How could she ever tell Harvey? All had changed and admittedly her heart broke because she had hurt the man she loved, betrayed the man she vowed to never betray. The mirror was her stark and quick reminder of how beauty had turned ugly and clean was now defiled. "How can I ever face him? How can I look at him again without insurmountable guilt? I'm so sorry Harvey!" She said as she cried while cleaning up in Brian's bathroom.

"Hey, are you all right in there?" Brian asked from outside of the door.

"Yes, I will be right out!" Stephanie said as she quickly wiped her tears. She wiped her tears faster and more vigorously. She attempted to apply makeup, but her tears smeared the face paint. Her hands shook as she brushed through her hair.

"Okay I will be here when you get back."

"I will be out soon!" Stephanie attempted to disguise the brokenness in her voice.

Stephanie finished up then walked into the living room where Brian was sitting.

"Took you long enough, but you look amazing." Brian said.

"Well thank you!" Stephanie put on her best smile.

"You're welcome! So, hey I was thinking that you should stay the night." Brian told Stephanie.

"Oh no I really do have to get home. It's almost two o'clock in the morning."

"I would really love to hold you all night and just be close."

"Perhaps another night, depending on where this goes, but tonight I must go home." Stephanie said definitively.

"Can I beg one more time?" Brian smirked.

"No, though your attempts were adorable!" Stephanie smiled.

They said their goodbyes. Stephanie made the commute home and now it was time to face the real music impatiently waiting. She slowly opened the door and crept into the house to avoid disturbing the tranquility of the house. She walked through the kitchen and into the living room. She was ready to make her way, slowly and quietly up the stairs. When suddenly the lights in the living room came on.

"Do you know what godda... motherfu..." Harvey composed himself and minded his language. "Do you know what time it is?" Harvey continued.

"Baby, can we please talk about this in the morning?" Stephanie asked.

"We cannot talk about this in the morning. We are talking about this now!"

"What's the difference Harvey?"

"Where were you?"

"I told you that I was going out with Julie. Baby please, please let's talk about this in the morning. I promise I will answer all your questions." Stephanie pleaded as she buried her head in her hands.

"Where the...were you?" Harvey asked.

Stephanie was quiet.

"Look over there!" Harvey pointed to the dining room table.

"Yeah, do you remember the song, *When I was Your Man*?"

There was dead silence in the room. "So now the cat's got your tongue?" Harvey paused, "Still silent?" See I bought you flowers! In fact, they sat there on that table for hours waiting to make you smile. I held your hand, or at least I tried. I bought your favorite candy and a heartfelt card because I..." Harvey touched his chest with his pointer finger, "...I love you and wanted to do something nice for you. Though it seems that while I was thinking of you, you were busy doing God knows what, with God only knows who!"

"Harvey I'm..."

"Seriously I do not want to hear your apologies or lies. I do not want to hear anything. For once I want you to just shut your mouth and listen. I've done nothing but love and respect you. I've treated your kids as if they were my own. Why were you out so late huh?" Harvey looked harshly at Stephanie.

"Harvey I was with Julie. We had a couple drinks and I just wanted to let the alcohol wear off enough for me to drive!" Stephanie tried to end the conversation on a light note.

"Whoa do not flipping lie to me like I am an inexperienced high school boy!" Harvey shook his head.

"I'd like to talk about this in the morning Harvey, I am really tired." Stephanie tried diverting the conversation again.

"You're tired? Ha! I do not care. I am tired from waiting up for your scandalous ass..." Harvey paused.

Stephanie interrupted. "Then baby let's go to bed. Let's hold each other and just be close...Please Harvey! I love you baby." Stephanie moved quickly towards Harvey and grabbed his hands.

"I do not want to touch you or be close to you. Who knows what you were doing tonight?" Harvey crooked his lips and looked Stephanie up and down.

"Nothing baby I promise! Just please hold me and kiss me. Harvey, I miss you." Stephanie began to silently tear up.

"Now you miss me?" Harvey asked cynically and rhetorically.

"Yes!"

Harvey paused, he understood that he still deeply loved Stephanie. However, his gut instinct told him she disrespected and disregarded their love and all that it meant to them. He sensed everything was soon to change.

Stephanie ran to Harvey and fell into his arms, "I love you, Harvey!"

Harvey held her for a moment then pushed her away, "Were you with another man tonight?" Harvey asked with a dark tone.

"No Harvey I promise!"

"You're lying to me!" Harvey pushed Stephanie away.

"Harvey, stop yelling, you're scaring me." Stephanie begged.

"Where is your phone?" Harvey's eyes began searching.

"Stop it Harvey!" Stephanie yelled and stomped her foot.

Harvey searched Stephanie's person for her phone, "Show me your phone." He demanded.

"Harvey everything will be alright in the morning. Let's just go to bed." Stephanie begged.

"No things will not be alright. Where is your phone?" Harvey asked again.

Stephanie clenched tight to her belongings.

Harvey felt all over Stephanie looking for her phone.

"Baby please, please stop this baby." Stephanie began to whimper.

"No!" Harvey said as he snatched her purse away from her. "Ah here it is." Harvey spoke of his small victory.

"Harvey don't do it; I am going to bed!" Stephanie began saying.

Harvey's eyes fluttered from anger and exhaustion. She lunged at Harvey and made one more attempt to stop him. Harvey pushed her away then went quickly to the bathroom and locked himself in.

"Who is Bianca?" Harvey asked.

"Just a friend from work babe." Stephanie responded.

"I've never heard that name." Harvey replied.

Harvey began to read the text message thread.

Brian- "Hey beautiful it was nice to see you again. I guess I better hang out at Julie's more often."

Stephanie- "It was nice to see you also."

Brian- "So I'd really like to get to know more about you."

Stephanie- "You're really handsome, but I do have an awesome boyfriend. He deserves my loyalty and respect."

Brian- "Okay well I kind of respect that, but I am coming for you beautiful because I usually get what I want."

Stephanie- "Oh is that right? Well we will just have to see about that, ha!"

3 DAYS LATER
Brian- "Hey you've been quiet. Is everything alright?"

2 DAYS LATER
Stephanie- "Sorry things are fine; I've just been busy."

Brian- "It's okay, I understand. When can I see you again?"
Stephanie- "You can't!"
Brian- "Why not?"
Stephanie- "Because I told you that I have a boyfriend."
Brian- "Then why do you text me?"

2 WEEKS LATER
Stephanie- "Hey!"
Brian- "Hey there beautiful stranger!"
Stephanie- "How have you been?"
Brian- "I've been good. I haven't stopped thinking about you."
Stephanie- "Oh really?"
Brian- "Yes!"
Stephanie- "So what have you been thinking?"
Brian- "Just about how I would really like to see you sometime."
Stephanie- "Well I am free this Saturday."
Brian- "I have something planned, but I can change my schedule to see you beautiful."
Stephanie- "Let's do it!"
Brian- "Can you meet me at the golf course in Penfield this Saturday in two days?"
Stephanie- "Yeah sure I can!"
Brian- "I am looking forward to seeing you.
Stephanie- "I am looking forward to seeing you also!"

Brian- "I hope you will be hungry afterwards."
Stephanie- "I am sure I can find a way."
Brian- "Well just seeing you will be enough. It doesn't even matter what we do."
Stephanie - "Likewise!"

Harvey blinked several times and wiped the crust from his eyes. He looked again and the messages were no longer there. He wondered if he had been dreaming or worse, hallucinating. Harvey put the phone in his pocket. He could not handle anymore. He walked out of the bathroom. Stephanie was sitting in the bedroom crying, but Harvey bore no compassion for her tears-Only fury for what had been done to him.

"Why? Stephanie, why?" Harvey yelled and stomped his right foot.

"Harvey, what the hell are you talking about. What has gotten into you lately?"

Harvey wiped the tears from his eyes, "You gave up Stephanie. You simply gave up."

"I think you're right, but I did not cheat on you." Stephanie responded as she shook her head.

"I wish you would have just talked to me." Harvey cried.

"I'm sorry!"

"So please be honest-who is he? And what happened tonight?" Harvey looked Stephanie directly in her eyes.

"There is no guy, I was literally having drinks with Julie."

"Darn it Julie!" Harvey crossed his arms and kicked the bedroom wall.

"I unexpectedly met Brian at Julie's house a couple of times when I was there, but again nothing happened."

"You expect me to believe that nothing happened?" Harvey said.

"Yes, baby I do!" Stephanie responded.

"Listen before things get worse, I am going to do what must be done." Harvey could not bring himself to look at Stephanie.

"Harvey please no..." Stephanie began to cry again.

"You have pushed me to the point of no return. Your begging does not motivate me to want to stay.

"Harvey, I love you so much, and I want this to work." Stephanie tried quickly wiping her tears, but more formed.

"I'm sorry also Stephanie. I tried to be the best man I could be. I tried to love you the way you desired. I really tried to make this work. I have remained committed. Even with your distance and going out so much I've stayed faithful, committed, and hopeful. Now I have lost all faith, all hope; its best that we break up." Harvey said as he choked back tears.

Stephanie grasped Harvey's arm tightly and cried one last cry, "Harvey don't go, please Harvey. I love you. I love you. Baby, I love you!" Stephanie was on her knees begging him to stay.

Harvey slept on the couch. He awoke early in the morning to plan where to go. Harvey walked into the 1st floor bedroom he once shared with Stephanie and shook her awake, "I am leaving!"

"Where are you going Harvey?"

"I don't know, I have to get away from you!" Harvey replied.

"Why are you leaving Harvey?"

"Is that a rhetorical question?" Harvey said as he walked towards the front door.

Harvey stopped at the door and walked back over to Stephanie; he helped her to her feet. Then he looked her in the eyes, kissed her forehead and said, "Stephanie, I will always love you and you will always have a special place in my heart, though loving you does not mean staying together is the right thing to do. Goodbye!"

Stephanie broke down in tears, "Harvey...Harvey...Harvey!"

Harvey was greeted unexpectedly. Ariana was standing at her bedroom door, "Are you leaving Mr. Harvey?" She asked as she wiped the crust from her weary eyes.

"Yes, and I am sorry!" Harvey tried to be brief and truthful.

"Aw will you be back?"

"I do not think I will." Harvey looked down. His hands shook.

Ariana's countenance saddened, "Why Mr. Harvey?" She whined.

"Because Mr. Harvey is sad and needs to be alone right now. Maybe you can come for piano lessons sometime."

"Well duh I'll be there for piano lessons, but I don't want you to go."

"I'm sorry Ariana, so sorry. Maybe one day I will see you again, but for now I gotta go." Harvey spoke through choked tears.

Ariana began to cry. Harvey walked over to her and did the best he could to leave her with something positive, "My dearest Ariana, sometimes people have to walk away so that everybody, including themselves, can be happy. I will never forget you and I need you to know that you did not do anything wrong. You are an amazing little girl and I wish nothing but the best for you. You see Ariana, there are times that bad things happen to good people. Then the good people have to leave so they can stay good."

They embraced, the moment was powerful and would never be forgotten. Harvey and Stephanie made eye contact when he turned away from Ariana's room.

"Har...!" Stephanie began calling.

Harvey continued walking towards the stairs. No words were spoken. He walked in the pouring rain back to his studio where he would stay for the night.

The most difficult thing about loving was letting go. Alfred Lord Tennyson said it best, "It is better to have loved and lost than to never have loved at all."

Harvey walked with conviction and confidence about his decision. His tears mixed with raindrops. He was a man rejected, dejected and changed by the circumstances of his life. He had loved and now he had lost, but was it better? Was he better? Or would all hell break loose. Only time could serve as the inevitable revealer of truth.

CHAPTER 23

Harvey sat on the couch in Larry's living room; he thought a lot about Stephanie. "Hey Larry!" Harvey called out.

"What's up?"

"I am about to catch up on some much-needed sleep bro."

"Stephanie loves you bro. Man, I really can't see her playing you like this."

"Yeah whatever. I'm going to take a nap. I am going to sit outside on the back deck to enjoy the sun."

"Give me a moment and I will join you."

"Thank you, but I need to be alone right now."

"Okay whatever you need Harv."

"I'll be outside if you absolutely need me." Harvey walked away.

Stephanie lamented over the loss of Harvey. She understood she had lost a good man. She understood past betrayal by a woman he loved deeply caused him to distrust her. Stephanie wished that

Harvey would have believed her to be different from Andrea.

Harvey was amazing and well, Brian was potentially the sum of what Harvey was not. Stephanie occasionally wondered if she should have given Brian a chance. That thought increased minimally with Harvey's absence.

Stephanie cried often. She wanted Harvey back, but somewhat understood why he could not feel the same. However, most days Stephanie sat mystified at Harvey's strong conviction concerning her infidelity.

Ariana and Johnathan were so big and steadily growing. When they smiled, she missed Harvey copiously more because often their smiles were the result of Harvey's interaction with them. Whether it was his compassion, his wit, his ability to be present when present, or Harvey just being Harvey which usually involved making others feel good. Jeffery was their father, but Harvey filled the position better than Stephanie could have. Women were not created to be fathers as men were not created to be mothers. Though similar in some ways, men and women are starkly different in enough ways.

Stephanie finally reached her lowest since Jeffery's death. Harvey had fallen off the grid. It had been almost two months since their breakup. Though at her lowest, love reached down and offered its hand. At the worst of recent times Brian stood before her offering better days ahead.

Much to Stephanie's surprise her phone began to ring. She did not usually answer calls from numbers unknown to her. Stephanie looked at her phone, put it back on the kitchen table and walked to the fridge to grab a drink of ice-cold water. She looked at Ariana and Johnathan playing in the front yard. Her children brought her a sense of great joy as well as relief. Stephanie feared the unborn child which she carried would be the cause of immense pain. Her fear was not merely focused on the physical ailments of childbearing. Stephanie presumed feeling the unborn move would prompt thoughts of Harvey and those late-night jabs and kicks would cause a more earnest craving for Harvey's presence.

Stephanie's phone began to ring again. She remembered the phone number from the call moments earlier. "It must be important!" She decided to answer. "Hello!"

"Hello, is this Stephanie?"

"This is Brian."

"Brian, Julie's friend?" Stephanie asked bewildered.

"Yes!" Brian responded in a very matter-of-fact manner.

"Um how did you get my phone number?" Brian could not see Stephanie's face, but she smiled a little because for a moment thought of Harvey ceased.

"I am sorry to inconvenience you, and please do not hate Julie, but she gave me your phone number."

"I am going to kill her." Stephanie mumbled.

"What did you say? Sorry, I could not hear you."

"Nothing!" Stephanie responded

"I know I am being very forward, and I have already crossed lines, but I would love to see you."

"I don't know Brian. Now is not really a good time in my life."

Brian began responding, but Stephanie did not register whatever he said because she was in the middle of texting Julie, "Why did you give Brian my phone number?"

"Girl, he wouldn't leave me alone about you and getting your digits so that he could talk to you."

"You should have asked me first!"

"Hello! Hello!" Brian called out.

"I am so sorry. I was texting."

"I will not take much of your time. Are you still seeing...What's his name?" Brian asked.

"Harvey, Harvey is his name and no he left me."

"Sorry, not too sorry Steph. Maybe you can tell me all about it over dinner."

"Yeah maybe. I guess text me some time since you have my number, creeper." Stephanie said with only a hint of sarcasm.

"Bye Stephanie." Brian decided not to engage in a war of words.

Several days passed and Stephanie continued communicating with Brian. Their friendship eventually grew. Six months had passed. Stephanie was slow to fall, but Brian was a good catch. Now she missed two men, but Brian was patient. He was more kind than expected. It took Stephanie longer than she thought, but eventually she was happy they had the opportunity to meet. She knew Brian would do anything for her. She thought about Harvey often. She knew she could not change the reality that Harvey no longer wanted her as part of his life or to be a part of hers. Stephanie didn't know if she would ever see Harvey again, but she wanted a chance to genuinely apologize for the pain he presumed she had caused.

Brian told Stephanie to take a chance, to leap and he would catch her. Stephanie told Brian to give her time because her heart hurt. Stephanie suppressed what she could but moved forward as best she could.

Brian and Stephanie had fun together. There was very little room for argument or stress because they were usually doing something adventurous, of course in moderation for the protection of the life growing inside of Stephanie. They took short trips, enjoyed cooking classes and art classes, family outings with the kids and many other things that brought them closer.

Stephanie needed time to get over Harvey before entering a new committed relationship. Stephanie pushed Brian away for fear of getting hurt, but he was persistent. Harvey was becoming a thing of the past. "Is your past ever really your past?" Stephanie wondered. And one thing remained true-she was carrying Harvey's child, and he was unaware.

CHAPTER 24

Harvey struggled to let go of Stephanie and the feelings he held for her. Their experiences, both good and bad, remained with him. He hoped to see her again. He didn't know what he would say or do, but he just wanted to see her once more.

Harvey heard about this new grocery store with cheaper prices than most other stores. So, he went. He only had to get a few items, but Harvey was always game for saving money. The lady up ahead visibly frustrated him.

"I just want to get my stuff and get out of here!" He thought. "Why do some people shopping needs to be an all-day event?" He asked himself.

The woman stood in front of one of the items that Harvey needed to get, "Excuse me ma'am..." Harvey began saying when the woman accidentally dropped her phone. He quickly ran around her to pick it up. Harvey stayed on one knee for what felt like minutes, "I know you from somewhere!" he said.

"I'm sorry Mr. uh...you do not look familiar." The mysterious woman responded.

"Harvey, my name is Harvey."

"Nice to meet you, Harvey."

"Are you sure we have not met before?" Harvey asked as he took a deeper look at the woman.

"Yes, I'm sorry I usually do not forget a face." The mystery woman replied.

"Okay well anyways ma'am I hope you have a good day. Can I sneak in here by any chance?"

"Yes, you can. And my name is Jenny." She eventually introduced herself.

"Thank you. Nice to meet you Jenny, I'm Harvey." He extended his hand for Jenny to shake.

Harvey grabbed his black olives off the shelf and moved quickly to the aisle immediately to his left. He turned the corner and it happened again. There was someone in front of him that looked like a person he had seen before. He wasn't prepared for more embarrassment though. He just continued his shopping. He grabbed what he needed from that aisle then turned around to continue shopping. He had forgotten to get ranch salad dressing. Now back in the aisle he was stunned at who stood in front of him, "Stephanie?" Harvey called out.

"Harvey?"

"You're...pregnant!" Harvey said surprised as instinctually he reached out to touch her stomach. He quickly retracted his hand.

"I am!" Stephanie smiled and nodded.

"With my kid?"

"Of course." Stephanie lowered her eyes and layered her hair behind her right ear.

"It's only been six months though." Harvey pondered. "How far along are you?"

"Almost 24 weeks." Stephanie responded.

"You haven't been with anyone else?"

"No, I have not."

"Okay well we should talk about this sometime."

"Yes, I agree." Stephanie half-smiled while surveying Harvey's non-verbal expressions; they left much to be deciphered.

"Anyways how have you been?" Harvey asked with a slight smile which communicated: I still love you; I still miss you and I wish things were different.

"I've been all right, but I really must go." Stephanie said as she struggled to smile. Deep inside Stephanie never stopped loving Harvey.

"Someone's in a hurry." Harvey joked.

"Sorry, the kids are being watched by someone and that person has somewhere to be." Stephanie responded.

"How are your..." Harvey began furthering the conversation.

"Harvey?" Stephanie interrupted. "I have to go." She continued.

"Okay well..." Harvey started saying.

"Bye Harvey!" Stephanie interrupted. "Let's talk about the baby sometime though."

Observing the back of Stephanie, Harvey said, "Yeah, uh...okay, I'll text ya."

Stephanie hurried away to hide the tears she was moments from shedding. She didn't think seeing Harvey again would cause as much sadness as it did. She confined her emotions enough to finish shopping. Stephanie finished shopping and loaded the groceries in the car. The tears eventually fell.

Harvey finished shopping and lingered in his car. He sat perplexed. "Unless she cheated on me then that is my child inside of her." He reasoned. "But why wouldn't she tell me?"

Harvey ruminated on the notion that Stephanie was carrying another man's child. He could not recall exactly how many months pregnant she was, but he wondered how she could conceive so shortly after he walked out. Harvey came to one resolve, "she cheated on me!" This angered Harvey; it saddened him just the same. For the first time in months Harvey broke down and cried. "How could she do this to me? She knows what Andrea had already done to me. I hate her...absolutely hate her!"

Harvey paced his studio trying to figure out how to confront Stephanie about his belief that she cheated on him. Nothing seemed to help with getting his mind off the past and likely betrayal. He decided that it was time to call. The phone rang and rang, but Stephanie never answered, "Stephanie this is Harvey. Please give me a call when you get a chance."

Harvey waited a few days before calling once more. Yet again. no response from Stephanie, "Stephanie I need to talk to you about something very important. Please call me at your earliest convenience." Harvey left a second message.

Stephanie was neither answering Harvey's calls nor responding to his messages; Harvey's rage further developed. "Stephanie this is my last message to you. Either that child you're carrying is mine or you cheated on me. Which one is it? Call me!"

"I really do not know why Harvey continues to call me." Stephanie said to Brian as they sat in Brian's car after leaving the arcade.
"I think that the guy just wants the truth."
"I really do not want to reopen that door. He's my past and I want to leave him right there." Stephanie grabbed Brian's hands and allowed their eyes to meet.
"You know I am right here Stephanie."
"I know Brian and you've been great. I cannot expect you to wait forever, but I am just not ready yet."
Brian turned slightly in the driver seat of his Maserati, "Stephanie all I am saying is you can wait to be over Harvey, or you can give me, give us a chance."

Tense silence filled the air.

"I will not wait forever." Brian continued.

"Really Brian?"

"Yes Stephanie!"

"Well in life there are consequences." Stephanie said as she looked away and out of the window.

"Okay so are you just going to ignore the guy?"

"I'd like to!" Stephanie responded.

"That's not a good idea-At all!" Brian said firmly.

"Welp, my choice."

"I mean you are carrying his child."

Stephanie stared out of the window, perplexed, confused, immobilized.

CHAPTER 25

Approximately six days passed since Harvey's phone calls. Stephanie hoped Harvey had gotten the hint and would leave her alone.

Stephanie went for a walk on the path she'd been walking for years. Harvey periodically took this walk with her. This intimate time together was invaluable to their relationship. Brian attempted to take the place of Harvey on these walks. On this day Brian could not join her because he had some work to catch up on regarding his real estate business. The sun was shining gloriously on this Saturday morning. Stephanie shortened her walk given the stage of pregnancy she was in. She walked about half of her normal route then turned to return home. Her walk was interrupted by an unlikely person. There they stood in the middle of the trail along the woods. Harvey was absolutely determined to get answers.

"Harvey come on. This is stalking. Why are you here?" Stephanie asked.

"I'm better at stalking than you can even imagine. Listen I deserve answers!" The look of death momentarily pierced Stephanie's soul.

"How did you even know I would be here?" Stephanie asked.

"You've walked the same route every Saturday for almost 12 months. You hardly ever changed your route."

"Okay but how did you know that I would be here today?" Stephanie asked as she moved further away from Harvey.

"I took my chances." Harvey responded as he inched closer.

"You're lying. Harvey, please leave me alone." Stephanie demanded

"Did you cheat on me?"

"No Harvey, now can you please just go?"

"You're the one lying now. How are you almost 6 months pregnant if you didn't cheat on me?" Harvey yelled and now stood face to face with Stephanie.

"You know Harvey, I am still in love with you; you're doing a great job of making me very grateful that we are no longer together." Stephanie said as she continued walking.

"I do not want to hear that. I want to talk about this child inside of you and we are going to talk about it!" Harvey said as he walked beside Stephanie.

"No Harvey we are not, and you really need to calm down." Stephanie responded as she paused to look at him briefly.

"You tell me to calm down when you're the one that compromised everything and still are?" Harvey posed the question that required no legitimate answer.

"Yes, I am telling you to calm down. You don't know what you're talking about."

"Don't tell me to calm down. How about you tell me the truth?"

"Bye Harvey! There's nothing to talk about. What we had is no more so please just leave it alone." Stephanie pleaded.

"There's obviously something to talk about because you're pregnant!"

"Yes, I am!"

"Which means you cheated on me!" Harvey exclaimed.

"No Harvey it doesn't mean that!" Stephanie replied. "I am sorry for any pain I have caused Harvey, but we really must leave the past in the past."

"Forget leaving the past in the past. What else could it possibly mean that you are pregnant in such a short time frame after you and I split?"

"It means that I am pregnant. Now I am leaving!" Stephanie attempted to walk away.

"You're a smart person, it means more than that. And you are not going anywhere until we are done with this conversation!" Harvey said as he blocked her path.

"Bye Harvey!" Stephanie said as she began to walk around Harvey.

"Don't walk away from me!" Harvey yelled as he stared at Stephanie.

Stephanie continued walking. She turned around and began walking backwards, "Bye Harvey!" She waved and lowered her head. She knew she still loved him and was still hurting by their untimely demise.

"Get back here!" He yelled. "I cannot believe her. She disrespects me yet again!" Harvey pounded his head and sat down on a nearby log.

Harvey sat on this log for what felt like forever. He didn't know how Stephanie could do this to him. He was hurting yet again. The sun began to set, and Harvey decided it was time to go home. He cried and screamed for what felt like hours. Harvey presumed this to be self-soothing, but with every tear his anger enveloped his conscience and soul; bringing him

closer to the conclusion he had to make
her pay. He had to make her hurt worse
than he hurt. Harvey knew somehow evil
had to prevail. He understood it was time
to submit to the evil which surged inside.
Revenge was the only noble recompense.
Daily Harvey prepared himself for the
moment evil would arise victorious and
wreak havoc on those deserving.

Harvey tried talking to Stephanie a
few more times, but she ignored every
attempt. He needed a reason for good to
win over the evil dancing alone beckoning
him to join.

Stephanie filed an order of
protection. Harvey didn't care, but his
consequence was a small amount of time
in jail. The story continued developing in
ways not in Harvey's favor.

What else could go wrong was the
mounting question.

CHAPTER 26

Harvey sat in his jail cell completely intent on minding his own business. He had never been to jail before. He only received a 60-day sentence since he had never been in trouble with the law before. Some days went much easier than others. Usually people left Harvey alone, until one day someone thought they had heard of him through a third party.

"Hey bro, aren't you that lame dude that used to date the girl my homie is chasing?" A much bigger guy said a few moments after Harvey stepped into the television room.

"Do not call me lame! It depends on who the girl is." Harvey responded with a dark and confident tone.

"My boy's name is Brian. I heard you were acting like a little puss chasing behind her months like a pubescent pleading for his first love to return!" The other inmate said.

"You do not know what you are talking about, so I suggest you leave me alone and mind your own business."

Harvey stepped a little closer. He remembered the year of kickboxing training and those hidden skills gave him a sense of confidence.

"Yo homie I will fuck you up. Who the hell you think you're talking to?" The much larger guy stepped into Harvey's face.

Harvey took a few steps back, "What Steph and I shared was real!" He was meek at heart and usually labored diligently to suppress the evil that sought manifestation.

"What Steph and I shared was real!" The other inmate mocked Harvey and laughed.

"What do you want?" Harvey asked.

"I want you to leave Stephanie alone. What you do to him, you do to me." The other inmate told Harvey as he pounded his chest with an open hand.

"What Stephanie and Brian share doesn't hold a torch to what her, and I shared."

"I may not have a master's degree or any other fancy degree that says I'm educated but bro the key words are 'share' and 'shared'! It's over!" The other inmate said.

"How do you even know all this man?" Harvey asked.

"I told you that Brian is my boy. He just came to see me last week. If I hear anything about you bothering her when you get out ima have my people do you filthy kid, I'm tellin ya. He showed me a picture of you that he got from facebook. He told me that you might be coming."

Harvey glared at the floor, looked up slightly and smirked. The other inmate laughed, and Harvey heard side chatter. By now he'd blocked external stimuli and focused on what he was feeling. Harvey remembered what his dad once told him, "Evil is real, it lives inside of us and sometimes it wins because we let it." Harvey's smirk curved and his eyes met the eyes of the other inmate.

"Okay tough guy. You want to go. I will give you first punch!"

"Sounds good!" The other inmate stepped into Harvey's face again.

Harvey stepped back and got into his fighting stance. The other inmate squared up.

"I'm ready for you man!" Harvey said.

The other inmate swung, and Harvey dodged the punch. "Wasn't even close." Harvey laughed.

"Stop it in there now before we beat both of you. Platt and you too Harvey, calm it down!" One of the Corrections Officer yelled with another prison guard by his side.

"I will see you in the yard." Platt, the other inmate said.

Harvey shook his head and sat down to write in his journal. He was receiving the surprise of his life. Harvey could have never imagined going through the things that he did behind bars. All in all, it greatly angered him that Stephanie had put him in such a god-awful place. "What we shared was real! I cannot believe all she has done to me. I guess everyone will hurt me in some way. Apparently big dude wants to kill me." Harvey shook his head.

Things were peaceful over the next few days. Harvey went into the recreation center to play a little basketball. Harvey showed off the moves he had learned over years of playing. The big Hispanic guy stepped into the room, "My crew got next."

Harvey recognized his voice, "Here we go again!" Harvey thought but continued to play.

"Yo you got some game for a white boy." Platt said.

"That's because I watch all the black players!" Harvey and his teammates laughed.

Pointing his right index finger, Platt spoke. "There's that little punk-ass dude right there that tried to step to me." Platt told his four homeboys that were with him.

"Hey bro let's go get him." One of Platt's friends said.

"Yeah, I'm definitely down to pound!" Another friend said.

"Yeah, me too!" The third friend said.

The fourth friend was quiet. He was a man of few words but proved himself lethal. William once told him, "It's the quiet ones you have to worry about."

The five of them walked over near Harvey. "We got next!" Platt said.

Harvey's team finished the game, winning by three points.

"I remember you, little puss!" Platt said to Harvey.

"Are you going to play some ball or stand over there talking nonsense?" Harvey wasn't afraid.

Platt walked over and stood within three feet of Harvey, "Nah dude I'm coming to talk my shit to your face."

298

Harvey dropped the ball and turned to face Platt. Harvey did not say a word. He just stood face to face with his unwanted opponent. Before long Harvey was face to face with Platt and all his crew.

"Really, five against one?" Harvey asked.
"Yeah!" Platt said. "That's how we get down!"
"And we about to make that face of yours a beautiful red if you know what I mean Casper." Platt's friend said.

Harvey took a deep breath.

"No, it's five against two!" One of Harvey's teammates said as he stepped closer.
"Don't you mean five against three?" Another teammate said, quickly stepping beside Harvey.
"Let's make that four, boys?" The teammate directly to Harvey's right said.
"I cannot leave my boys out there being down one so it's five against five."

They stood face to face, and it was time for battle. "Let's do this mono-e-mono!" Harvey said.

"You ready black?" Platt asked.

Harvey turned to his teammates, "I'm pretty sure I'm white..." They all laughed as he turned back to Platt.

Much to his surprise Platt released a punch. Harvey tried to dodge the punch, but Platt's punch connected with the right side of Harvey's head. "I am about to knock this white boy out yawl!" Platt laughed.

Harvey stumbled back, then readjusted his shoulders. He smirked, then flinched at Platt. He did not bat an eye, but also did not figure that Harvey was efficient in martial arts. Out of nowhere Harvey snap kicked Platt's left knee. Platt buckled, then yelled, "Motherf...ugh!" He lunged towards Harvey and tried to grab him. Harvey side-stepped to the right then stung Platt with a one-two punch combination. Platt stepped back, faked with his left then hit Harvey with a right hook after Harvey flinched. Harvey stumbled once more. Platt stepped in and hit Harvey with a left uppercut. Platt threw an overhand right and Harvey slipped the punch, hit Platt with a left hook then a jab, then a right hook. Platt swung a right hook. Harvey moved in closer, shortening the distance. He hit Harvey with a left uppercut, another right hook then Platt grabbed Harvey, and they began to tussle. Harvey bit Platt's hand then pushed him back. While Platt was stumbling Harvey kicked Platt in the stomach, punched him twice in the face. Platt ducked the third punch then quickly slammed Harvey to the floor!

"Break...it...up!" The Corrections Officer yelled.

The crowd dispersed and the powers that be could not rightfully punish anyone; the large crowd quickly dispersed rendering identification impossible.

Harvey's time in jail was nothing short of difficult, adventurous, and enlightening. The two men had a few more altercations, but no more physical fights occurred. He demanded that Harvey stay away from Stephanie and the kids. Harvey firmly let Platt know that he had zero authority to tell him what to do. Harvey told Platt that Brian was lucky he did not find and punish him for causing so much drama. Platt said that whatever Harvey does to Brian, or anyone associated with Brian is being done to him as well. Harvey said so be it.

Platt admired Harvey's courage but could never tell him. "That kid most definitely has crazy heart!" Platt would periodically tell some of his fellow inmates.

Harvey's time was winding down. Sitting in that jail cell more hours and days than he cared to count gave him ample time to think and to plot his next move. Harvey looked in the mirror minutes before being released and thought, "evil is real, it lives inside of us and sometimes it wins because we let it." He smiled.

CHAPTER 27

Harvey went to the place he did his best thinking, his studio. He sat behind his piano where he once found solace. No songs emanated. His fingers had lost the desire to create the glorious sounds once produced. All the things in life that once brought meaning were no longer important.

All his friends had abandoned him, or at least it appeared that way to Harvey. He thought often of Andrea and Raina. She broke his heart and there was nothing he could do about it. Or so he thought. He ruminated about Stephanie frequently. She broke his heart, but Harvey no longer felt powerless.

Harvey's anger spiked when he saw Brian with Raina and discovered he was her real father. Several months prior Harvey began focusing on truly making peace with his past and the demons therein. Andrea apologized repeatedly. She never truly wanted to lose the love shared with Harvey. She did not intend to hurt him.

303

Andrea met Brian at a bowling alley one night when out with her friends. He was with his friends, only a couple of lanes away. She was attracted to Brian. He was forward and Andrea had a weakness for men with bling; Brian was iced. They exchanged numbers. Andrea believed she could keep Brian in the friendzone despite his interest in her. Sometimes the most dangerous concoction is covert emotion and overt connection. Opportunity ignites the fire.

A few weeks passed and Andrea decided to meet Brian at a bar with a couple of friends. Amidst the girl chatter she said, "I'd sleep with Brian if I were single...Or if no one would find out," she laughed. The night carried on, Andrea had a few mixed drinks and when the night ended, she left with Brian. Harvey was out with 3 of his friends playing pool and Andrea knew the approximate time he would be getting home.

Harvey decided it was time to call Andrea again.

"Please pick up." He pleaded with Andrea and the incessantly ringing tone. She did not answer.

Harvey's phone began to ring, "Hello."

"Hi Harvey, it's been a while since I heard from you." Andrea said.

"I know. I just really needed to talk."
Harvey scratched his head.

"Okay I have a few minutes."

"So, you said a guy named Brian is
Raina's father, correct?"

"Yeah, why are we having this
conversation though?"

"I haven't forgiven you just yet,"
Harvey said with a slightly sinister laugh.

"I really do hope you find love
Harvey; you truly deserve it."

"If I deserve it then why didn't you
respect our love?"

"Harvey, I made a mistake."

"A mistake that costs us." Harvey
replied.

"You are right Harvey, okay! Is that
what you want to hear? I am so sorry that
I hurt you, but you know what?"

"I'm listening."

"Okay do not be rude." Andrea
expressed her frustration.

Silence!

"Anyways!" Andrea continued. "No
one is perfect. I cannot ever change what I
did to you, to us, to Raina, but I was
willing to try."

"There are some things that simply
cannot be forgiven."

"You see Harvey, that's just it, you're wrong. Forgiveness is a choice, resentment and bitterness, also a choice.

"So now you're qualified to counsel me?"

"Harvey, you haven't changed much. You're still difficult and stubborn. Did I mention argumentative?"

"Can I see Raina?" Harvey sounded desperate.

"I'm afraid that is not a decision to be made after one phone call. It has been over a year since she has seen or talked to you."

"At least she has her daddy, Brian."

"If only he was interested in being involved in her life."

"What? What a deadbeat! Listen it was nice to talk to you again. Maybe we can grab coffee or a bite to eat sometime." Harvey made a feeble attempt at reconnecting.

"I will think about that. Thanks for calling."

"Bye for now." Harvey lowered his phone to press the end button. When he heard a voice.

She teared up when talking to Harvey on the phone. It had been a while since they spoke, and she realized how much she missed him and took their love for granted.

"Hey Harvey, Harvey."

Harvey looked at his phone screen. "Yeah Andrea?"

"Take care of yourself. Love without limit. Forgive for the sake of happiness. Last, but not least, you're a good man. Let love win. Let the goodness inside of you overshadow all else. That's your ticket to happiness."

"Thank you." They hung up the phone.

Silence gripped the moment. "Let's hope it's not too late." Harvey surveyed the walls in the room where he sat alone.

Blinded by anger and rage, Harvey missed the sadness in Andrea's voice.

Brian was now responsible for taking two potential children away from him. Harvey was a man robbed of fatherhood, two times over, by one man. It angered him even more that Brian was not involved in Raina's life. Harvey viewed himself a gentleman who treated others the way he wanted to be treated. Even more reason the hurt he experienced angered him so vehemently. Harvey was a good man, but as Psychologists says, hurt people, hurt people. He embodied good and hated evil. However, with all the pain he'd experienced, evil began to appear more appealing than good, and wrong more pleasing than right. Grace was no longer Harvey's motto. For the first time in his life Harvey was convinced of this: evil was real, it lived inside of him, and it would win because he was willing to let it.

Unfortunately, Harvey now knew pain was a part of life and not something he could completely avoid. Harvey thought about all the lessons his parents taught him: lessons of respect, generosity, honor, dignity, integrity, and authentic love. He thought about Andrea's recent words, *"Take care of yourself. Love without limit. Forgive for the sake of happiness. Last, but not least, you're a good man. Let love win. Let the goodness inside of you overshadow all else. That's your ticket to happiness."*
Those lessons were now at war with the evil surging inside of Harvey. What would be the calculated collapse? Life presented Harvey with two choices-take revenge or forgive! Once again Andrea's words came to mind, *"Forgive for the sake of happiness."*
His greatest dilemma: 1) Obey his moral compass; 2) Succumb to the evil surging from within!

It was now three o'clock in the morning and Harvey moved from the studio to his car. "I'm a good man and that will never change."

What Harvey did not say is: though he was good man, even good people could not escape evil.

It had now reached 3:17 AM. Harvey sat in disarray and more contemplative than ever before. The day of reckoning had arrived; the battle between good and evil was the greatest that Harvey had ever faced. He looked up at the moon and stars hoping for direction. The clouds changed.

Harvey cranked his engine and began the pursuit to rid himself of the evil wrestling the very core of who he was. The commute began.

Harvey now sat outside of Stephanie's house. Where love laid and hate awaited a shift in the emotional experience.

Momentarily the stars stood still. The galaxies slept. The Heavens warned while Hell rejoiced, and for the final time the moon and stars wept.

From Harvey's perspective this day of atonement.

"But I am a good man!" Harvey reasoned within himself.

"Harvey, you must make her pay. Not just her, but you must make them all pay!" He told himself, "All of them!" Harvey concluded.

Harvey paused, "I will catch up to you as well Brian, you damn bastard! You think you can just rob me of happiness twice over and never pay for it? Ha! You're sadly mistaken. I will show you!"

Harvey looked up at the water hitting the windshield as Heaven cried out. He now stood outside of the car. The rain drenched the exterior; his tears stained the inside. As the water fell from his face and hands, his anger rose, coalescing with evil.

"This is the day of atonement!" Harvey walked a little closer to Stephanie's house.

With each step his conviction plagued his decision. "Do not let evil win Harvey-Not today and not this way!" Harvey wiped the water from his brow.

It took Brian forever to leave, but eventually he did after his home alarm system was compromised. Brian did not want to leave Stephanie alone. Contrary to popular opinion, Brian truly was a good friend.

Harvey knew Brian's address because he followed him home one night after running into him at the local park.

The thunder roared; the Heavens' anger intensified. Harvey stepped with increased ambivalence, but nevertheless, forged ahead.

"You must make them pay Harvey- All of them. Every...last...one!" The voice of destruction said.

The winds rocked Harvey from side to side. His shoes were now brown from the mud in the front lawn. His hair reeked of mildew.

The time had almost arrived. Harvey placed his right foot on the step of the front porch. "The time has come!" Evil told Harvey.

"But you're a good man, and good men do not purposely hurt people." The voice of reason took the moment captive.

"But Harvey, she cheated. She betrayed your love. Even worse she did these things with a guy that robbed you of your first chance at fatherhood. Kill them, Harvey! Leave no witnesses my 'conduit'. I have great faith in you Harvey!" Evil delivered its next pitch.

"As do I have immense faith in you Harvey. Evil only wins if you let it!" The voice of reason made another attempt at the preservation of good.

"Hey there Harvey! They deserve to hurt like you hurt, only worse!" Evil demanded recompense for their sins.

"Shut up! No!" Harvey tried to close the door that evil continually pushed through.

"End those motherfuckers Harvey-End them!" Evil became more forceful.

Good was losing. Harvey's moral compass was failing. Moral law was becoming a thing of old, and the law of natural consequences tainted Harvey's subconscious mind.

Harvey stepped onto the front porch and the memories of the life shared with Stephanie flooding his mind, catapulted by the offense which destroyed the love they shared, the love he adored, and the love he'd given his all for.

"You have the power, Harvey! There are two choices-You can forgive, or you can exact revenge on your offenders. I can do no more! The force will not be with you." The voice of reason/Good offered its final plea.

"God, you created evil. Even worse God, you placed evil inside of me, so you must understand!" Harvey reasoned. "You created Lucifer, the Angel of...I thought Angels did not have wills of their own! Yet he gathered an army and rebelled against

312

you; Your own minister of music tried taking the kingdom you created. Yeah, God you created evil. Thanks a lot!" Harvey said angrily while looking up at the sky. "I am made in your image after all!" Harvey laughed.

Harvey paused, "*Let love win.*" He remembered Andrea's words. "No!"

Harvey raised his right foot to step forward when Andrea's voice resounded audibly, "*Forgive for the sake of happiness.*" Harvey shook his head. "Shut up Andrea, shut up!" he yelled. Stephanie turned from her left side to her right but continued sleeping.

"My only happiness comes from succumbing to hate and the evil within me." Harvey reassured himself then took a few steps closer to the door.

Harvey stood on the front porch, "I was born in sin and shaped in iniquity! Surely, I was sinful from the time my mother conceived me!" Harvey shook his head from side to side, "Heavenly father please forgive me for my sins. It is not I, but the evil within me which you have created that is exacting vengeance." He looked up into the sky, "God, my God...Forget me not!" He cried.

The moon and stars stared at Harvey. Heaven collided with earth evil finally claimed the victory. Deeper darkness fell upon the earth; thunder roared.

Harvey reached for the door, but quickly retracted as he began hearing voices. He remembered words of wisdom from his parents, lessons from his friend Larry, but most debilitating words of the moment were from Andrea," *"Let the goodness inside of you overshadow all else. That's your ticket to happiness."*
Harvey began to wail then quickly wiped his tears. "I refuse to listen to you Andrea." Harvey remembered the words of his father, "Evil is real, it lives inside of us and sometimes it wins because we let it." Harvey made his decision.

Harvey picked the lock and quietly stepped inside. He had to walk past the kids' room to get to Stephanie's room. He stopped and stared inside. Johnathan slept peacefully as if he had not one care in the whole wide world. Ariana tossed and turned in her sleep. Harvey adored Ariana and was sad about the hurt to come.
He walked over to Stephanie's room and looked at her sleeping. She clenched her pillow. When Harvey first thought to

harm her, positive memories returned. The memories were a moment or so late because he had already succumbed to the evil within him.

"Get up now!" Harvey demanded.
"Brian, is that you?" Stephanie asked sleepily.

Harvey's anger intensified, "No! No! No! Harvey hit himself in the head repeatedly... "No! It's Harvey."
"Am I dreaming?"
"Oh no 'babe' it's me, Harvey in the flesh at 3:48 in the morning." His demeanor resembled the room: dark with little light.
"Harvey I am going to call the cops and you're going back to jail. Please leave right now." Stephanie demanded as she quickly sat up in bed.
Stephanie felt around the bed and nightstand to the left of the bed, "Looking for this?" Harvey said as he showed her cell phone which he grabbed while she was asleep.
"Harvey what are you doing? Give me my phone!"
"You're going to pay for hurting me. Did you know that Brian is Raina's father? I am keeping the phone you used to hide your works of iniquity."

"No, I didn't! Harvey, you look like a demon, pure evil. I swear I did not cheat on you, not even once!"

"Well, he is Raina's father, and I am going to make him pay for ruining not one but two chances for me to be a father."

"Harvey it is almost four in the morning. I need you to get out of my house now." Stephanie demanded.

"Actually, you and I are going to the basement so that we do not wake up the kids!"

"No, we are not. I am going to sleep, and you are leaving." Stephanie spoke with conviction.

"Wanna bet?" Harvey asked as he flashed his gun.

Stephanie gasped for air, shocked, "I will do what you want, but Harvey this is crazy stuff you only see in books or movies."

"Maybe your story will end up as a best seller or lifetime special feature." Harvey said in a stoic manner.

"I do not know what you want, but please put that gun away. And what's in your duffle bag?"

"To the basement now!" Harvey spoke firmly while maintaining extremely low volume.

"Okay! Okay!" Stephanie said as she placed both feet on the floor.

Harvey followed Stephanie into the basement. "Sit down in one of these chairs." Harvey ordered.

Stephanie trembled with fear, "Harvey please stop!"

"Sit...down!" Harvey spoke a little louder and more harshly.

"No Harvey, I won't do it." Stephanie shook her head and cried a little.

Harvey flashed his gun.

"You will just have to shoot me Harvey."

"So be it!" Harvey said as he raised the gun and aimed at Stephanie's head.

Time froze...for just a moment.

"Ah!" Stephanie screamed, "Harvey!" She cried and backed towards the chair.

"Now sit...the...fu...down!" Harvey yelled. "Ugh I really do not want to lose my religion in here."

"There is no religion in you!" Stephanie yelled and leaned forward.

"If I tell you one more time to sit down, I am going to end you just like evil told me to." Harvey gripped his gun and duffle bag tighter.

"Oh no Harvey, my sweet Harvey you have gone mad." Stephanie said as some of their past arguments were now explicable. "Have you been taking your medications as prescribed? I was faithful to you and would never betray you." Stephanie tried to be strong, but she was more afraid in this moment; more than she's ever been.

"Why are you calling me that?" Harvey said in a normal tone of voice. "Why are you calling me that?" Harvey yelled. "Why are you calling me that?" Harvey's voice decreased in volume. Harvey paced back and forth in front of Stephanie, "Why are you calling me that?" He whispered, then threw his bag onto the floor. He paced, "Why the fuck are you fucking calling me that?" Harvey yelled.

"I'm sorry! I'm so sorry Harvey." Stephanie apologized profusely.

"You're not sorry!" Harvey said as he pulled Stephanie by the hair. "Now..." Harvey yanked Stephanie into the chair, "Sit down!"

"What are you going to do to me?"

"You will find out when I do it!"

"Mommy! Where are you mommy?" Johnathan asked as he walked into her bedroom, then began walking down the stairs.

"No! No! No! I said no kids."

Stephanie looked around, confused. "Who is he talking to? Who is talking to him? This is not good." She was so afraid.

Harvey wacked himself in the head with the gun.

Harvey chuckled oddly, "This is lovely-two for the price of one!" He smirked.

"Harvey you wouldn't hurt my kids."

"Are you sure about that?" Evil beamed inside of Harvey.

"Please Harvey. Please do not hurt my child!" Stephanie begged.

"Hey, it's not my fault the kid woke up!" Harvey justified his ensuing actions.

"Harvey I will do anything, just please do not hurt my child!" Stephanie begged as her butt was now on the edge of the chair.

"Okay shut up. You caused this to happen." Harvey yelled and walked towards the duffle bag.

"Harvey..."

"Mommy!" Johnathan called out from the kitchen which was right above the basement.

"Tell him you're down here!" Harvey demanded and began opening the duffle bag.

"I will not do it Harvey! Absolutely not!" Stephanie replied. Her tears fell faster and faster and fear gripped her soul.

"You're in no position to be stubborn but I get it. I'll tell him. Hey Johnny boy she's down here." Harvey yelled in a high pitched and inviting voice.

Harvey quickly tied Stephanie's hands behind the chair with the rope he brought. When she tried to fight back, he shoved he pistol into her back.

"Mommy?" Johnathan said groggily as he walked down the basement stairs.

"Over here hun."

"Yep, over here Johnathan." Harvey said.

"Mommy why are you sitting in the chair like that?"

Harvey looked in his bag and grabbed one clear substance and one bottle of a multicolored substance, then pulled out his needle.

"Harvey what are you going to do?" Stephanie asked.

"Something completely unforgettable, ha! But do not worry you will get to watch it all, then your fun or should I say your misfortune will start." Harvey smirked.

"Harvey please stop. I will do anything." Stephanie pleaded.

"Johnathan are you tired?" Harvey asked.

"Yes, but I want my mommy."

Harvey ignored Johnathan and began filling the needles with the various substances that he pulled out of his bag. He smiled, then looked up at Stephanie. The fear in her eyes served the longing of

Harvey's soul quite well. He looked at Johnathan with such compassion, but he had to pay for the sins of his mother...

"I'm sorry Johnny boy, but that will not be possible!" Harvey said as he yanked Johnathan over to him and plunged the needle into his neck. The multicolored substance incinerated his veins.

Johnathan's pulse slowed at an increasingly alarming rate. His heart worked less until cardiac arrest became the recompense for the sins of his mother, "For the wages of sin is death!" Harvey justified the process he'd began.

"No! No Harvey! Please tell me that you did not just kill my little boy." Stephanie fought hard to free her hands and get out of the chair.

"Shut up Stephanie." Harvey said in a low voice. He paused, then yelled, "I do not want to hear your goddamn begging and pleading. You had your chance, and you blew it. Now blow me! On another note, don't bother. I have a better plan for you." Harvey grabbed his needle and grabbed Stephanie's neck. "You know what. I will wait. I want you to watch your son's demise. Maybe he is sleeping, but maybe you will never know. Is sleeping or is he dying right before your cheating eyes?" He looked at his watch, "Tic-toc, tic-toc." Sinister laughing emanated from Harvey.

"Please Harvey." Stephanie's begged and pleaded increased.

"Shut...up!" Harvey said as he smacked Stephanie, "I told you I did not want to hear you begging and pleading! You had your chance, and you missed your opportunity, and you know what? Sometimes life does not offer second chances. Call Brian!" Harvey said.

"No!" Stephanie replied.

"No?" Harvey asked in a surprised tone.

"I said no Harvey! He is a friend who has nothing to do with this." Stephanie cried.

"You are not in the best position for negotiating. Now call Brian!" Harvey yelled.

"No! No! No! No! Harvey, please help my son. If you call 9-1-1 right now, I will tell them a stranger did this." Stephanie spoke through tears and shortness of breath.

"Okay since you're being difficult then I will call him. That guy will pay for his sins also. I am so sorry Stephanie, but you did this to little Johnny boy." Harvey pulled Stephanie's phone out of her bag and dialed Brian's number.

"Hello." Brian said groggily as he answered the phone at 4:35 in the morning.

Harvey did not say a word. He just let Brian hear Stephanie screaming.

"Oh my-gosh. What is going on? I will be right there." Brian said as he threw on a pair of sweatpants, a t-shirt, some shoes, grabbed his keys then quickly headed for the door.

"Now that Brian's on the way. Say your final goodbyes!"
"Brian, Brian...You are a great guy and I hope you find..."
"Fuck your decree of love! Enough, I am not listening to that sappy sack of shit. It's over and tomorrow you will open your eyes in Hell. Whores don't go to Heaven."
"I'm confused!" Stephanie said as she cried beholding the sight of her beloved son withering away. There was no one to come to his defense.
"And to you little one inside of this...woman-I'm sorry you had to pay for the sins of your father!" Harvey felt a kick. "Feisty already!" He laughed, "Well it's too bad the world will never get to see that endearing trait of yours." Harvey punched Stephanie in the stomach.

Harvey suddenly stopped, *"Let the goodness inside of you..."*

"I already told you to shut up Andrea."

"No Harvey, I 'm Stephanie. I think you're hallucinating again."

Harvey took quick and heavy breaths then hastily cleared his forehead of the perspiration that gathered. "Do not speak!" Harvey yelled.

Stephanie closed her eyes. For she knew her time had come! She wept.

The thunder roared and Heaven sent its anger to earth. The wrath of God sat without justice; the love of God watched without action.

As the rain began to pour once again, Harvey stuck the needle into Stephanie's neck. He delivered the clear substance into her body. Stephanie's pulse slowed at an increasingly alarming rate. Her heart worked less until cardiac arrest became the recompense for her sins, "For the wages of sin is death!" Harvey justified the process he had begun.

"Harvey?" Stephanie called out.

Stephanie closed her eyes as Harvey said, "I have loved you and now I have lost you, but it is better to have loved and lost than to never have loved at all. "I guess Alfred Lord Tennyson was good for something after all." I will not apologize, for your sins have led you to the death you deserved. I love you! Goodbye my sweet, sweet Stephanie!" Harvey began to cry, rubbed Stephanie's hair, kissed her lips then quickly wiped his tears.

The moon darkened and the stars hid their splendor. Harvey reveled in his glory as he walked upstairs to look at Ariana, "I could never hurt you, but I'm so sorry for what you will awake to tomorrow." Harvey's tears soaked his soul. His wrath had been satisfied.

Harvey walked down the stairs. He poured a little gas in the basement and struck a match. He walked outside and left the front door open. He gassed the outside of the house and set it ablaze. He walked into the dark of night with light from the fire casting an inverted heroic shadow. Harvey had satisfied the evil within. But his conscience could not rest with what had been accomplished. Failure still felt like the ultimate result of a job left unfinished. He dialed 9-1-1 from Stephanie's phone then tossed it in the bushes.

Brian drove down the street doing 85 miles per hour in a 35 mile per hour zone. He jumped out of his car and ran as fast as possible towards the house.

Harvey smiled, then pulled out his gun. He ran towards Brian, pointed his gun, cocked back then something happened-he stopped. He stood idle, and he had no clue as to why. Harvey stood as a man rejected, yet a man revived, a man forsaken and yet fulfilled. The tears poured like the rain from above and Harvey, as he walked away, said, "evil is real, it lives inside of us and sometimes it wins because we let it."

Harvey stood outside of his car in the pouring rain. He quickly jolted his head to the right then took 3 steps away from the car door. He quickly turned around. He heard the screams and suddenly felt compassion. *"Take care of yourself. Love without limit. Forgive for the sake of happiness. Last, but not least. You're a good man. Let love win. Let the goodness inside of you overshadow all else. That's your ticket to happiness."* Andrea's words returned.

Harvey sat on the ground and a plethora of thoughts and images emerged. Harvey had flashes of Stephanie and Brian that quickly faded. Harvey's heartbeat increased. His time in jail quickly disappeared from his conscious mind. Harvey's hallucinations became stronger. The image of Brian at Julie's house disappeared from Harvey's reverie. The images of Stephanie and Brian crumbled like dust and surfaced as a figment of his imagination. Platt faded as an illusion of vision. The text messages Harvey read between Brian and Stephanie suddenly seemed like storied fiction. "What have I done?"

Harvey realized Stephanie's innocence was much more likely than her presumed guilt.

Harvey remembered dumping his pills down the drain. "Stephanie did not betray me. Was Stephanie carrying my child? Did I...?" Harvey began to regain his grip on reality. "But I saw her talking to a guy at Julie's house. She was always on her phone. She did stay out late at times or was I imagining that too." Harvey walked towards the house then he heard sirens.

"Evil is real, it lives inside of us and sometimes it wins if we let it." Harvey recited the anthem sought to bring immense joy. "I succumbed to evil and good lost the war. I ignored the timely words of Andrea. I chose hate, for the sake of happiness. Revenge so sweet now bitter, I can taste my demise. My ticket to happiness is on a train soon departing to

Hell." Harvey collapsed to his knees then put the gun to his right temple, "Please forgive me." Harvey stared at the ground watching the water drip from his hair. "I will always love you, Andrea. Stephanie I am so sorry. I could not see what was truly in front of me. I hope one day you and the kids understand that I was simply acting out my sickness. I am not well and for that I cannot apologize; I am forever apologetic and indebted for the way my illness made you pay for sins not committed." Harvey put his finger on the trigger, "Goodbye mom. Goodbye dad. I am underserving of my next breath. I wish I was never born. Mom mental illness ran in your family. Why did you even have children? I will fix this mistake." Harvey lowered the gun and pulled a bullet from his pocket. He looked at the gun then at his shaking hand. He loaded one bullet into the chamber. "Mom, you ridiculed me profusely when dad was not home. You scalded me in places where dad would never see because only you bathed me. In your younger years you left me home alone to party with your friends when dad temporarily worked overnight shifts. I was only five years old." Harvey put the gun back to his right temple. "Dad you should have been more present, but I know you loved me. Andrea, you really messed me up. I love Raina more than life itself."

Harvey began slightly pressing the trigger. "I hope my ghost haunts you. Stephanie, you were the only woman that never hurt me. I am pathetic. I am undeserving. I am demented. My strength is failing. I am evil and goodness has fled. I am...dead!" Harvey felt Ariana's hand touch his and the gun.

Ariana looked back at the house aflame and took a deep breath. She knew she had to be strong. She heard sirens getting increasingly louder. "Good is better than evil Mr. Harvey and love is better than hate."

The fire truck pulled quickly to the side of the road; the paramedics were not far behind. The passenger jumped out of the van swiftly and beheld the scene before his eyes. "Mister..." he paused and sweat began to profusely form on his face... "Don't!"

Harvey paused, "Evil is real, it lives inside of us and sometimes it wins because we let it." Harvey yanked his hand away from Ariana. Ariana stumbled back while holding onto Harvey's hand. Harvey's arm in motion, Ariana falling; Harvey wrestled to dissect the complexities plaguing his brain, but nature had a

course. The gun finished what its master
started. Bang!

www.ingramcontent.com/pod-product-compliance
Lightning Source LLC
Chambersburg PA
CBHW060941120726
47910CB00002B/427